Samuel French Acting Edition

Agatha Christie's Murder on the Orient Express

adapted by
Ken Ludwig

SAMUELFRENCH.COM   SAMUELFRENCH.CO.UK

ISBN 978-0-573-70773-5

www.SamuelFrench.com
www.SamuelFrench.co.uk

FOR PRODUCTION ENQUIRIES

UNITED STATES AND CANADA
Info@SamuelFrench.com
1-866-598-8449

UNITED KINGDOM AND EUROPE
Plays@SamuelFrench.co.uk
020-7255-4302

Each title is subject to availability from Samuel French, depending upon country of performance. Please be aware that *MURDER ON THE ORIENT EXPRESS* may not be licensed by Samuel French in your territory. Professional and amateur producers should contact the nearest Samuel French office or licensing partner to verify availability.

MUSIC USE NOTE

IMPORTANT BILLING AND CREDIT REQUIREMENTS

MURDER ON THE ORIENT EXPRESS was first produced by McCarter Theatre Center in Princeton, New Jersey on March 14, 2017. The performance was directed by Emily Mann, with sets by Beowulf Boritt, costumes by William Ivey Long, lights by Ken Billington, sound by Darron L. West, dialect coaching by Thom Jones, and wigs by Paul Huntley. The production stage manager was Cheryl Mintz. The cast was as follows:

HERCULE POIROT	Alan Corduner
MONSIEUR BOUC	Evan Zes
MARY DEBENHAM	Susannah Hoffman
HECTOR MACQUEEN	Juha Sorola
MICHEL THE CONDUCTOR / HEAD WAITER	Maboud Ebrahimzadeh
PRINCESS DRAGOMIROFF	Veanne Cox
GRETA OHLSSON	Samantha Steinmetz
COUNTESS ANDRENYI	Alexandra Silber
HELEN HUBBARD	Julie Halston
COLONEL ARBUTHNOT / SAMUEL RATCHETT	Max von Essen
DAISY ARMSTRONG	Ivy Cordle

MURDER ON THE ORIENT EXPRESS was co-produced by Hartford Stage Company in Hartford, Connecticut on February 15, 2018. The performance was directed by Emily Mann, with sets by Beowulf Boritt, costumes by William Ivey Long, lights by Ken Billington, sound by Darron L. West, dialect coaching by Thom Jones, and wigs by Paul Huntley. The production stage manager was Samantha Flint. The cast was as follows:

HERCULE POIROT	David Pittu
MONSIEUR BOUC	Evan Zes
MARY DEBENHAM	Susannah Hoffman
HECTOR MACQUEEN	Juha Sorola
MICHEL THE CONDUCTOR / HEAD WAITER	Maboud Ebrahimzadeh
PRINCESS DRAGOMIROFF	Veanne Cox
GRETA OHLSSON	Samantha Steinmetz
COUNTESS ANDRENYI	Leigh Ann Larkin
HELEN HUBBARD	Julie Halston
COLONEL ARBUTHNOT / SAMUEL RATCHETT	Ian Bedford
DAISY ARMSTRONG	Jordyn Elizabeth Schmidt

CHARACTERS

HERCULE POIROT

MONSIEUR BOUC

MARY DEBENHAM

HECTOR MACQUEEN

MICHEL THE CONDUCTOR

PRINCESS DRAGOMIROFF

GRETA OHLSSON

COUNTESS ANDRENYI

HELEN HUBBARD

COLONEL ARBUTHNOT

SAMUEL RATCHETT (doubles with Colonel Arbuthnot)

HEAD WAITER (doubles with Michel the Conductor)

SETTING

The principal action of the play takes place aboard the Orient Express as it travels from Istanbul to Western Europe.

TIME

1934

ACT I

Mid-day to morning

ACT II

Morning to mid-day

A NOTE ON THE USE OF MUSIC IN THE PRODUCTION

In the world premiere co-production of *Murder on the Orient Express* at McCarter Theatre Center and Hartford Stage Company, in 2017 and 2018 respectively, the producers licensed copyrighted music, listed below under Original Production. Professional groups are urged to make an attempt to license the same music in their own productions.

For the purpose of this publication, and for groups intending to produce the play without the additional cost of licensing copyrighted music, the songs listed under Acting Edition may be used in their place.

ORIGINAL PRODUCTION	ACTING EDITION
Act I, Scene Two	
"Anything Goes" by Cole Porter	"I Want to Go Back to Michigan" by Irving Berlin
Act I, Scene Two into Act I, Scene Three	
"The Dance of the Knights" from Sergei Prokofiev's ballet *Romeo and Juliet*	The "Vorwärts Drängend" passage from Gustav Mahler's *Symphony No. 1*
Act I, Scene Five	
The first twelve lines of "The Lullaby of Broadway" by Harry Warren and Al Dubin	The first ten lines of "Swanee" by George Gershwin and Irving Caesar
Act I, Scene Eight into Act I, Scene Nine	
Samuel Barber's overture to *The School for Scandal, Opus 5*	Approximately two minutes into Gioachino Rossini's overture to *La Gazza Ladra*

All other music referenced in the script is out of copyright. Each licensee is responsible for their own research.

ACT I

Scene One

(In the darkness we hear a train coming toward us. It begins quietly then builds to a roar of sound and light. It's as though a huge, powerful train is hurtling past us at breakneck speed.)

(Silence.)

(Then we hear a domestic scene unfold in the blackness in front of us. We hear the voices, but we cannot see the participants.)

MOTHER. Goodnight, sweetheart. It's time for bed.

LITTLE GIRL. Do I have to, Mama?

FATHER. Just listen to your mother.

*(The **NANNY** is a kind, loving woman in her thirties.)*

THE NANNY. But who's tucking you in?

LITTLE GIRL. The wolf?

THE NANNY. Noooo.

LITTLE GIRL. The bear?

THE NANNY. Noooo.

LITTLE GIRL. My nanny!

THE NANNY & LITTLE GIRL. *(Laughter and tickling.)* Yaaaaay!

THE NANNY. Now up we go.

*(During the following, we hear the **LITTLE GIRL** and her **NANNY** run up the stairs and into the **LITTLE GIRL**'s bedroom. We hear the door open, then close behind them.)*

LITTLE GIRL. Faster, faster! You're a train, you're a train!

THE NANNY. Daisy Armstrong!

(Tickling, laughter. They're in the room.)

Now straight into bed and no more nonsense.

LITTLE GIRL. Oh, all right.

*(She gets into bed. The **NANNY** sits beside her.)*

THE NANNY. Close your eyes. Night, night.

*(The **NANNY** exits. We hear the door open and close. A beat of calm, and then we hear a deep, ominous sound, like the bass note of an organ. Light from the hallway spills into the room, and we see the shadow of a hulking man entering the room. Perhaps we see the **LITTLE GIRL** as well.)*

LITTLE GIRL. Who are you? Go away. *Nanny!*

THE MAN. Come!

LITTLE GIRL. No! I won't! I won't come! Mama! Daddy! AHHHHHHHHH!

(Her scream turns into the scream of a train whistle, as the train goes past us again with another roar. Vrooooom!)

*(Steam from the train billows out across the stage. Out of this mist, **HERCULE POIROT** walks into view and addresses the audience.)*

POIROT. Good evening. The story you are about to witness is one of romance and tragedy, primal murder, and the urge for revenge. What better way to spend a pleasant evening together?

From the beginning it was an odyssey of deception and trickery. One minute I could see the light, like the beam of a train engine hurtling past. The next minute, all was darkness and the thread that I pulled came away in my fingers and led to nothing.

I believe it was the greatest case of my career, but who am I to say? Modesty forbids it. It was certainly the most difficult I have ever encountered, and it made me question the very deepest values that I have held since I was a young man.

(Middle Eastern music is heard.)

It began in the exotic city of Istanbul. I planned to vacation there for several days following a trying case that was on my nerves, but things began changing the moment I stepped into the dining room of the world famous Tokatlian Hotel, where the enormity of the prices was matched only by the self-esteem of the waiters. My name, incidentally, is Hercule Poirot and I am a detective.

Scene Two

(We hear a small hotel band playing "I Want to Go Back to Michigan" by Irving Berlin. **POIROT** *bows slightly and now we are in the dining room of the Tokatlian Hotel in Istanbul in 1934. The* **HEAD WAITER** *escorts* **POIROT** *into the room.)*

HEAD WAITER. This way, *monsieur.* I have a beautiful table that I'm sure you will enjoy. It is *monsieur's* first time in Istanbul?

POIROT. That is correct. How did you know?

HEAD WAITER. Ohh, I have my ways, *monsieur.* My little observations. In this business, one needs to be a detective, like that famous Poirot fellow who comes from France.

POIROT. I believe he is Belgian.

HEAD WAITER. No, no. From France. I know him personally.

POIROT. Ah.

HEAD WAITER. Your table, *monsieur.*

POIROT. *Merci.*

(As **POIROT** *sits and takes up a newspaper,* **COLONEL ARBUTHNOT** *bursts the dining room and hurries over to a table where* **MARY DEBENHAM** *is waiting. The* **COLONEL** *is a Scotsman with a Scottish accent in his mid-thirties, handsome, and very matter-of-fact.* **MISS DEBENHAM** *is an English beauty in her late twenties. There is a sadness, however, around her eyes. She is anxious.)*

ARBUTHNOT. Mary. There you are!

MARY. James! At last! Where have you been?!

ARBUTHNOT. Oh, I'm not that late, am I?

MARY. Of course you are. You're always late. And I was terrified we'd miss the train. It would ruin everything!

ARBUTHNOT. I was just exploring a bit. I've never been to Istanbul before and I quite adore all this eastern nonsense.

MARY. Well, I don't. I just want to leave right now and get it over with.

(**ARBUTHNOT** *puts his hand on her cheek.*)

ARBUTHNOT. I wish to hell you were out of all this. You deserve better, you know.

MARY. Shh! Not now! No one should see us like this. Not till it's all behind us. Besides, I think we're being observed by that funny little man over there.

(*She nods toward* **POIROT**, *who is hidden behind his newspaper.*)

ARBUTHNOT. What, him? He's just some damned foreigner who probably doesn't even speak English.

(**POIROT**'s *newspaper gives an involuntary shake.*)

MARY. Shall we order? I'm starving.

ARBUTHNOT. Not here. I found a cute little place around the corner where I'm sure the food will be ten times better.

MARY. But we can't be late for the train! We can't miss it!

ARBUTHNOT. We won't be late, I promise, now stop fussing and come on, let's hurry.

(*As they go, we notice* **MRS. HUBBARD** *sitting nearby. She is an outspoken American in her fifties, well-dressed with a touch of flamboyance, and she calls to the* **HEAD WAITER** *as she rummages through her handbag for her money.*)

MRS. HUBBARD. Yoohoo! Excuse me, waiter. You did a very nice job and I'm leaving you something extra because of it.

(*At this moment, we notice* **HECTOR MCQUEEN** *sitting at one of the tables. He is a nervous*

*young American in his thirties with a
strained, rather beleaguered face.)*

MRS. HUBBARD. Excuse me, young man. Are you American?

MACQUEEN. Y-yes I am.

MRS. HUBBARD. I thought so. I can see from your passport.
Us Americans have to stick together, you know.
Especially in a place like this. I can't even pronounce
half the things on the menu. Can you believe it? And
what's a falafafafafafel? I keep seeing them on the street
and they look like you could play hockey with 'em.

MACQUEEN. I believe they're made of fried chickpeas.

MRS. HUBBARD. Well there ya go. Who knew? Some people
will fry anything. By the way, I don't mean to snoop
but I see your train ticket sitting there on the table and
I wonder – do you know if they're providing a bus to
the station?

MACQUEEN. I don't think so. I-I believe the hotel has a
private car.

MRS. HUBBARD. Well don't you worry, I'll ask and find
out. As the Bible says, "If Moses doesn't know the
answer, ask the concierge." Now I better go. I think I'm
annoying that odd little man with the silly moustache.
(Sotto voce.) And I don't think it's real.

> *(As **MACQUEEN** and **MRS. HUBBARD** exit,
> **MONSIEUR BOUC** enters. He sees **POIROT**, his
> face lights up and he chuckles happily. He
> taps **POIROT** on the shoulder. **BOUC** is another
> Belgian, a young middle-aged man of good
> humor.)*

BOUC. I hope that the food at this humble establishment is
up to your usual standards.

POIROT. What? What's this?... Ah, *mon Dieu*, it is *Monsieur*
Bouc!

BOUC. My friend! Haha!

POIROT. *Mon ami!* But what are you doing here?

BOUC. What am *I* doing here? This is my city! I live here!

POIROT. Of course, I'm a fool!

BOUC. I run Wagon-Lit, the greatest train company in the entire world, and the central office is in this hotel. *Garçon!* This meal is on me, please charge my office.

POIROT. *Ah non.*

BOUC. *Ah oui.* It will give me pleasure, you are my guest here. So tell me, what are you doing here? You are solving a crime, eh?

POIROT. No, no, I did that last week in Syria. It was a bad affair. An army officer, a missing check, a beautiful woman, puh. It did not end well.

> (*As* **POIROT** *describes the case, a* **MAN** *appears in a blue down light, wearing an army tunic and an officer's hat. We are witnessing* **POIROT***'s memory.*)

The man was guilty, that was certain. But perhaps, because I pressed the man too hard to admit his guilt...

> (*The* **MAN** *raises a pistol to his temple and fires. Bang! The noise is startling. The* **MAN** *collapses and fades away.*)

It was unfortunate in the extreme. And yet I believe I did nothing wrong.

BOUC. Of course you did nothing wrong. If you break the law you must pay the price. That is what *you* have told me.

POIROT. It is what I live by.

BOUC. Now tell me, you are staying here at the hotel?

POIROT. I was hoping, eh? I was going to play the tourist, but at the desk there was a telegram from Scotland Yard, begging me to return at once, so I have asked the concierge to get me a ticket for tonight on your famous Orient Express.

BOUC. There will be no problem, and the best news is, I will be joining you, for I go to Lausanne tonight on business.

POIROT. Haha! *C'est magnifique.*

(The **HEAD WAITER** *approaches* **POIROT.***)*

HEAD WAITER. *Pardon, monsieur.* The concierge said to tell you there are no more first class tickets for the Express tonight. It is sold out.

POIROT. *Ah non!*

BOUC. *Attends.* It is my train and it is never sold out at this time of year. That is ridiculous.

HEAD WAITER. It must be a party, or a convention, perhaps.

BOUC. Well, you tell the concierge to find a berth for *Monsieur* Poirot. He is my personal friend.

HEAD WAITER. But *monsieur* –

BOUC. The number seven is always available. It is held in reserve. Now go tell him!

HEAD WAITER. Right away, *monsieur.*

(He exits.)

POIROT. *Merci.*

BOUC. It is nothing. A gesture. Now you see this menu? Throw it away. Tonight we shall sit on the train together, just like old times, and we will dine like kings.

POIROT. The food on the train, it is edible?

BOUC. *Monsieur* Poirot! You stab me in the heart! I am writhing on the ground at your feet! It is not a mere train that will carry you tonight, it is a legend. It runs like no other vehicle on the earth. The fittings are from Paris, the paneling Venice, the plates are from Rome, and the taps from New York. The best food, the best beds, the best pillows, the best feathers inside the pillows. It is poetry on wheels, and Lord Byron himself could not write it better. *Monsieur*, prepare yourself. In one hour, I will meet you on the platform of the Orient Express.

(Suddenly we hear the "Vorwärts Drängend" passage from Mahler's Symphony No. 1. *The dining room disappears, the scene changes, and the ominous, powerful music takes us into the train station at Istanbul.)*

Scene Three

(The platform is full of steam and smoke and is throbbing with activity. In the background we glimpse the sleek, shining body of the Orient Express gleaming with romance. The greatest train in the world is about to accept its passengers and sail out of the station.)

(At the center of the activity is **MICHEL,** *the conductor. He is a good looking Frenchman, about forty, with a quiet, almost grave sense of humor. He has a clipboard in hand listing the names and compartments of the passengers. Meanwhile, we hear an announcement over the loudspeaker.)*

ANNOUNCER. *Messieurs et mesdames, l'Orient Express partira dans vingt minutes du quai numero dix. Veuillez faire attention aux marches, soyez prudent et bon voyage.* Ladies and gentlemen, the Orient Express will depart in twenty minutes from platform ten. Please watch your step and have a safe trip.

(Bells and whistles sound as **PRINCESS DRAGOMIROFF** *enters like a galleon in full sail with a woman named* **GRETA OHLSSON** *in her wake. The* **PRINCESS** *is in her seventies. She is Russian, expensively dressed and heavily bejeweled.* **GRETA,** *by contrast, is Swedish, with a Swedish accent. She is in her thirties and plain. There is a frightened, sheep-like quality about her. She is carrying three or four suitcases and struggles with them.)*

PRINCESS. Greta, will you please put those suitcases down, you are driving me mad!

GRETA. No, no, princess, do not have concern, they are not so heavy as they look, I am sure.

PRINCESS. They are extremely heavy!

MICHEL. Princess Dragomiroff. How lovely to see you. *(To* **GRETA***.)* Please, let me help you, *madame.*

> **(MICHEL** *relieves* **GRETA** *of the luggage.)*

GRETA. It iss *mademoiselle.* I am not married, except to God almighty who lives in heaven.

> *(She crosses herself.)*

PRINCESS. Oh Greta please, not *now. (To* **MICHEL***.)* This is Greta Ohlsson.

GRETA. I am a missionary and I verk in Africa with little babies.

PRINCESS. I have agreed to pay her way if she will assist me as I travel to Paris.

MICHEL. But your usual companion, Miss Schmidt –?

GRETA. She iss very sick.

PRINCESS. The doctors are calling it a cardiac event, but she is German so it is very unlikely to slow her down.

GRETA. I vill pray for Miss Schmidt and God vill protect her.

PRINCESS. Greta, please, that is enough, just get on the train.

MICHEL. You are in compartment eleven, princess, as usual. *(To* **GRETA***.)* And Miss Ohlsson, you are sharing with a Miss Mary Debenham in compartment four.

> **(MARY** *enters, dressed stylishly.)*

MARY. I'm Miss Debenham.

MICHEL. Ah, *mademoiselle.* You will be sharing with Miss Ohlsson here.

GRETA. I vill do my very best so I am not disturbing you.

MARY. Oh, I'm sure we'll get along just fine.

> *(At which moment,* **SAMUEL RATCHETT** *appears. He's a middle-aged American businessman, brusque, unforgiving, with a threatening demeanor, and a whiplash of a voice.)*

RATCHETT. *Hector!*

MACQUEEN. Here, sir. I-I'm right here.

RATCHETT. Is the luggage on board?

MACQUEEN. Yes sir, it is. And I-I checked this morning for any mail that might have arrived overnight, and-and this came in apparently –

RATCHETT. *(Reading.)* Goddammit!

MACQUEEN. I know, it's *awful.* I mean just look at this! "Prepare to *die*"?

RATCHETT. Keep your voice down!

MACQUEEN. You should call the police!

RATCHETT. It's none of their business.

MACQUEEN. But these are dangerous! This is the third one you've had in a week.

It's good you have a *gun.*

RATCHETT. *Would you keep your voice down!*

> *(By this time,* **POIROT** *has entered and approached* **MICHEL***.)*

POIROT. Excuse me. Could you direct me to compartment number seven, please.

MICHEL. Number seven, *monsieur*? I believe there must be some mistake.

POIROT. Let us hope not. I must get to London by the end of the week. My name is Hercule Poirot.

MICHEL. Hercule Poirot, the detective?

> *(Heads turn.* **POIROT** *is a celebrity.)*

RATCHETT. Well, what do you know! Hercule Poirot! I've heard o' you. You're famous.

POIROT. *Merci, monsieur.*

RATCHETT. The name is Ratchett. Samuel Ratchett. Import-export. And I may have some business for you.

POIROT. I'm afraid I am on vacation, *monsieur.*

RATCHETT. Oh, you'll change your mind when you hear the price. Eh? Haha!

MICHEL. *Monsieur* Ratchett, you are in compartment two.

(**RATCHETT** *doesn't like being interrupted.*)

RATCHETT. I *know* where I'm going, thank you. *(To **POIROT**.)* We'll discuss it inside.

CONDUCTOR. *(Offstage.)* All aboard!

(**BOUC** *enters in high spirits.*)

BOUC. *Monsieur Poirot! Alors.* You have beat me to the gate. You have met Michel? He is from Paris and he is the best conductor in the company!

MICHEL. *Merci, monsieur.* But your friend says that he has number seven, and I'm afraid it is taken. Indeed, the entire first class coach is full.

BOUC. That is incredible.

MICHEL. I know, *monsieur.* All the world elects to travel tonight.

BOUC. You will put him in number one, please. *(To **POIROT**.)* It is my personal compartment. I will find something in one of the other carriages.

POIROT. *Non, non.* I cannot take your bed, *mon ami.*

BOUC. I insist, it is done. Michel, you will make the arrangements.

POIROT. I am in your debt.

BOUC. Now tell me, have all the passengers checked in with you?

MICHEL. Not yet. We are waiting for a Mrs. Hubbard and the Count and Countess Andrenyi.

BOUC. *(To **POIROT**.)* I hear that the countess is one of the greatest beauties of Europe. She is Hungarian, I believe, a commoner, who became a doctor, and when she married the count she became royalty!

MICHEL. I see her coming.

> (**COUNTESS ANDRENYI** *sweeps in carrying a small makeup carrier. She is in her twenties, brilliantly beautiful and dressed to the nines in furs and diamonds. Her hair and makeup are impeccable, and she has a warm smile*

*that wins you over immediately. She is out of
a fairy-tale.)*

BOUC. Countess Eléna Andrenyi! Welcome! I am *Monsieur*
Bouc of the Wagon-Lit.

COUNTESS. *(With a Hungarian accent.)* I am delighting to
see you.

BOUC. Your reputation precedes you, *madame.* May
I present my friend, *Monsieur* Hercule Poirot.

COUNTESS. The famous detective. That is being wonderful.
I have read about you in the papers, *monsieur,* and
I admire you greatly.

POIROT. *Ön nagyon kedves.*

COUNTESS. *Ez as igazság.*

POIROT. *Nagyon örvendek.**

COUNTESS. You speak Hungarian beautifully.

POIROT. Not as well as you speak English.

MICHEL. May I help you with your bag, *madame*?

COUNTESS. No, no, it iss nothing at all.

BOUC. And your husband the count is coming?

COUNTESS. *Hèlas,* he cannot join me this trip. But since
I am visiting my mother it works out nicely. He does
not like her.

    (Offers her hand.)

Monsieur Poirot, I look forward to hearing of your
wonderful adventures.

POIROT. *(Kissing her hand.)* And I look forward to telling
you about them.

MICHEL. Compartment twelve, countess.

    (The **COUNTESS** *sweeps away, into the train.)*

BOUC. I think you are in love, my friend.

POIROT. I will not discount this possibility.

---

* POIROT: You are very kind.
COUNTESS: It is simply the truth.
POIROT: It is an honor to meet you.

(At this moment, **MRS. HUBBARD** *blows onto the platform.)*

MRS. HUBBARD. Is this that Orient Express I keep hearing about? It doesn't *look* that impressive, at least not from here.

MICHEL. You are Mrs. Hubbard?

MRS. HUBBARD. Mrs. Helen Caroline Peabody-Wolfson-Van Pelt-Hubbard, if you please, from the beautiful garden state of Minnesota. Mr. Peabody, my first husband, was a very good soul but the poor man had no talent for longevity, and I shouldn't say poor because he did very nicely for himself, thank you very much. My second husband was a Mr. Wolfson who I loved rather dearly, but he loved a lot of women and so I traded up and got a Van Pelt, but I caught him in bed with that redhead from the Waldorf who did his nails. Then at last I found Mr. Hubbard and I call him my little white knight for saving me from a life of bridge games and watery cocktails at the Minneapolis Country Club.

BOUC. And is Mr. Hubbard joining you?

MRS. HUBBARD. No, Mr. Hubbard is not joining me. Mr. Hubbard and I traveled together once and he said it raised his blood pressure. I don't know why. So now I do it for both of us. *(To* **MICHEL.***)* Do you like to travel?

MICHEL. I travel every day.

MRS. HUBBARD. Then you and I should exchange notes some time.

MICHEL. Compartment three.

MRS. HUBBARD. Is that yours or mine?

MICHEL. Yours, *madame.*

MRS. HUBBARD. I hope it's comfy.

MICHEL. I have never had a complaint, *madame.*

MRS. HUBBARD. I'm sure you haven't.

(She exits.)

POIROT. She is quite the character.

BOUC. They are all characters. If I was Balzac, I would write a novel about all of them.

POIROT. And just think: for three days these strangers are brought together in the closest of quarters, eating and sleeping under a single roof.

BOUC. And then at the end they part, never to see each other again.

POIROT. Unless, unless.

BOUC. Unless what?

POIROT. Unless there is an accident. Or something fatal occurs.

BOUC. *Monsieur* Poirot! Why do you say such a thing?!

POIROT. Forgive me. It is my business. And I sense that something is wrong – that there is a tension among these passengers of yours. One of them does not fit in. It makes me frightened.

BOUC. Oh, *monsieur*! No more business, please. You must now succumb to nothing but pleasure – and prepare yourself to step aboard the pride of the company Wagon-Lit for the most memorable journey of your entire life!

(We hear the hoot of the train whistle: and as they head for the train, we hear the second movement of Mahler's Symphony No. 1 *ring out majestically and with romance.)*

(The train bells clang, there is a blast of steam, and the set changes to the interior of the Orient Express. The change is dramatic and magical.)

Scene Four

(We are now in the Art Deco dining car of the first class coach of the Orient Express. The car gleams with elegance and romance. The fittings are gold, the cushions are made of red plush, and the bar in the dining car is fashioned of inlaid wood with an Art Deco depiction of an elegant woman lying across an ottoman. It is worthy, in its way, of the great mosaics in Ravenna. The train is breathtaking.)

*(A number of **PASSENGERS** come through with their luggage.)*

MRS. HUBBARD. Well, ain't this the bee's knees. Maybe I'll just move in for good.

MICHEL. This way, please, and watch your step.

MRS. HUBBARD. Holy cow. Is it snowing out there?

MICHEL. We get a lot of it this time of year, I'm afraid. Last year we got stuck in the snow for seven days.

MRS. HUBBARD. *Seven days!* Was there liquor on board?

MICHEL. There is always plenty.

MRS. HUBBARD. Well, now I can breathe again. Don't get me wrong, I also eat solid food as long as it's cooked in bourbon. As they say in the movies, lead on, MacDuff!

*(They exit as the **PRINCESS** and **GRETA** enter.)*

PRINCESS. Greta, you must keep up, keep up! We have to get settled in before the train starts moving!

GRETA. I have to confess to you, princess, that I am not liking trains since I am little girl. They are feeling very tight to me, like clothing that is made wrong size and is squeezing my bosom, may God forgive me.

PRINCESS. Oh, don't be silly. Trains are wonderful.

GRETA. I am also not liking the strangers and der clickety-clackety. But ve vill be sitting next to each other, *ja*? That part iss good. In Africa once I am on a train and there is noise and crying and animals and oh! And I look up from my book and sitting there next to me, right on the seat, iss a very old goat. Haha. Is true. *Old goat!* He is like my companion. And on this trip that we are taking together right now, I think it will not be so different, *ja*?

> (**GRETA** *exits. The* **PRINCESS** *reacts and follows her off as* **POIROT** *enters, followed by* **RATCHETT,** *who is trying to catch up with him.*)

RATCHETT. Mr. Poirot, slow up! Now I'd like to discuss that proposition I mentioned.

POIROT. *Non, non,* I'm afraid it is not a good time.

RATCHETT. Oh sure it is. Sit down. I'll be quick, I promise.

POIROT. I am afraid –

RATCHETT. Sit down.

POIROT. ... *Eh bien.* Proceed.

RATCHETT. Now I want you to take on a job for me.

POIROT. I take on few new cases.

RATCHETT. You'll take this one on, I guarantee it.

POIROT. And why is that?

RATCHETT. Because I'm talkin' big money here. Mr. Poirot, I have an enemy.

POIROT. I would guess that you have several enemies.

RATCHETT. Now what is *that* supposed to mean?

POIROT. You are successful, *n'est-ce pas?* Successful people have many enemies.

RATCHETT. Right. That's it exactly! You see I've been getting some threatening letters lately and I want an extra pair of eyes to do some snoopin' around. And that's what you do, am I right? Snoopin'? Of course, I can take care of myself.

> (*He flashes the gun under his coat.*)

But I'll pay you five thousand dollars. How does that sound?

POIROT. *Non.*

RATCHETT. All right, ten. For a few days' work.

POIROT. I am not for sale, *monsieur*. I have been very fortunate in my profession and I now take only such cases as interest me – and frankly, you do not interest me.

RATCHETT. You want me to grovel, is that it?

POIROT. I want nothing, *monsieur*, except to leave.

> (**POIROT** *exits.* **RATCHETT** *is darkly unhappy. He stomps his foot. After a beat, the* **COUNTESS** *enters, passing through. She nods as she tries to go past him.*)

COUNTESS. Pardon me. Sorry.

RATCHETT. Hey, you're that countess, aren't you?

COUNTESS. That is correct.

RATCHETT. Well, you're awful pretty. And from what I hear, you were a commoner to start with, just like the rest of us.

COUNTESS. That is also correct.

RATCHETT. So does that mean you'll have a drink with me?

COUNTESS. I am married, *monsieur.* My husband is having business elsewhere. Please excuse me.

RATCHETT. Now not so fast.

> (*The* **COUNTESS** *looks up sharply, but he's blocking her way. There is something threatening about him.*)

COUNTESS. Move out of the way, please.

RATCHETT. Hey, you don't need to get all high and mighty about it.

COUNTESS. If you do not move this second I will scream.

RATCHETT. *Just wait a minute!* You've said that you're unattached at the moment, and we are on a train, so who the hell's gonna know what happens in some private room on some two-bit piece o' –

(Whap! She slaps him very hard across the face. His instinct is to spring forward and attack her back.)

COUNTESS. Stay away from me.

*(**MACQUEEN** bumbles into the room.)*

MACQUEEN. Oh Mr. Ratchett, I've been looking for you. I-I put your glass of wine next to your bed, and if you don't need anything else tonight, I thought I'd just –

RATCHETT. *Shut up, Hector. Just shut...up!*

*(At which moment, **BOUC** enters.)*

BOUC. Aha. My friends. I hope that you are settling in all right and enjoying yourselves? It won't be long now until –

(Kerchunk! The train lurches to a start, and everyone grabs something nearby. It begins to roll and there is a sense of relief.)

Haha! Not long at all! The journey begins, and I wish you both good luck and godspeed!

(The lights fade quickly and we hear the train begin to roll, haltingly, then faster and faster until it's shooting along the tracks.)

(Zooom! Clang, clang, clang! Hoonk! Hoonk!)

(As the train moves, we see the snow falling, getting heavier by the second.)

(Simultaneously we hear the frantic, propulsive opening of Rachmaninoff's arrangement of Rimsky-Korsakov's "The Flight Of The Bumblebee.")

Scene Five

(We now see three adjoining sleeping compartments lined up next to each other. From the audience's perspective: **POIROT***'s compartment is on the left,* **RATCHETT***'s compartment is in the center, and* **MRS. HUBBARD***'s compartment is on the right.* **POIROT** *and* **RATCHETT** *share a common wall with no connecting door.* **RATCHETT** *and* **MRS. HUBBARD** *share a common wall with a connecting door.)*

(When the lights come up, we see **POIROT** *and* **RATCHETT** *in their respective compartments getting ready for bed.)*

*(***POIROT** *takes meticulous care of his hair and moustache and folds his clothes with precision.)*

*(***RATCHETT***, on the contrary, is annoyed with everything, growls unhappily, and takes a large, unhappy swig from a glass of wine.)*

(Meanwhile, **MRS. HUBBARD** *has picked up her telephone and is buzzing* **MICHEL***. Bzzzzzz! Bzzzzz!)*

MRS. HUBBARD. Hello?! Hello?!

(We hear **MICHEL***'s voice through the receiver.)*

MICHEL. *(Offstage.) Oui, madame?*

MRS. HUBBARD. *(Opening her door.)* Michel, could you bring me a bourbon, please. And put it on the rocks. The tap water's terrible.

MICHEL. *(Offstage.)* Right away, *madame.*

MRS. HUBBARD. And how about some nibbles?

MICHEL. *(Offstage.)* Nibbles, *madame?*

MRS. HUBBARD. Munchies. Yummies. Things to snack on while I drink my bourbon.

MICHEL. *(Offstage.)* Ah, you mean like crisps, *madame.*

MRS. HUBBARD. Yeah, like crisps. We call 'em nibbles in the midwest. Have you ever nibbled on anything, Michel?

MICHEL. *(Offstage.)* I have not had that pleasure, *madame.*

MRS. HUBBARD. Well, you bring me those crisps and I'll give you a lesson. Over and out.

> *(She hangs up, then looks in the mirror.)*

You're not doin' so bad there, kid. You're lookin' younger all the time. Ha!

> *(She turns on her radio, hears a tune she likes, and starts to sing and do a dance routine. She's surprisingly professional. The more she sings, the louder she gets.)*

I'VE BEEN AWAY FROM YOU A LONG TIME
I NEVER THOUGHT I'D MISSED YOU SO
SOMEHOW I FEEL
YOUR LOVE IS REAL
NEAR YOU I LONG TO WANNA BE

THE BIRDS ARE SINGIN', IT IS SONG TIME
THE BANJOS STRUMMIN' SOFT AND LOW
I KNOW THAT YOU
YEARN FOR ME TOO
SWANEE! YOU'RE CALLING ME!

> *(We now see **RATCHETT** in the compartment next to her. He's livid and bangs on the wall.)*

RATCHETT. Would you keep it down!

MRS. HUBBARD. Shut up! Who asked you?!

RATCHETT. It's the middle of the night!

> *(Bzzz! Bzzz! **RATCHETT** is buzzing for the attendant, and **MICHEL** hurries down the corridor.)*

MICHEL. Sir, what is it?!

RATCHETT. Would you tell that ridiculous woman in there to keep it down, it's time for bed!

MRS. HUBBARD. *(Calling in to* **RATCHETT***'s room.)* Ridiculous woman? I heard that!

MICHEL. *Monsieur*, if the lady wants to sing a little song –

RATCHETT. It is twelve o'clock at night!

> *(***MRS. HUBBARD*** *barges into* **RATCHETT***'s compartment through the connecting door.)*

MRS. HUBBARD. Now listen you, just mind your own business.

RATCHETT. Stay out of here! This is my compartment!

MRS. HUBBARD. If I want to enjoy myself, I'm gonna do it, so just pipe down.

RATCHETT. You're insane, you're just... *Get out!*

MRS. HUBBARD. What are you, a thug? Are you in the mafia? Michel, I think he's dangerous.

> *(Seeing* **RATCHETT***'s gun on his night stand.)*

Oh my God, he's got a gun! Michel, it's a gun!

MICHEL. It is not against the law, *madame*.

RATCHETT. Get out this instant!

MRS. HUBBARD. You must be crazy!

RATCHETT. I said get out!

> *(She walks out, slamming the door behind her. Bang!)*

> *(Lights down in* **RATCHETT***'s compartment. The moment* **MRS. HUBBARD** *is back in her room, she starts singing again and doing the Charleston, just to annoy him.)*

MRS. HUBBARD.

CHARLESTON, CHARLESTON,
MADE IN CAROLINA!
HEY MR. WHOSITS! I HOPE YOU DON'T HAVE
ANY TROUBLE WITH THIS ONE. IT WOULD BE
    UN-AMERICAN!

SOME DANCE, SOME PRANCE
I'LL SAY THERE'S NOTHING FINER

THAN THE
CHARLESTON, CHARLESTON...

(As she continues singing, we see pinpoint spotlights on three of the **PASSENGERS**.*)*

POIROT.

Oh là là, it will be a long night.

BOUC.

She will ruin me, it is all over.

PRINCESS.

Someone should shoot her and put her out of her misery.

(Lights out quickly.)

(In the transition light we see the snow falling, getting heavier and heavier. The wind is howling, blowing the snow sideways.)

(Zooom! Hooonk! Clang, clang, clang! The train rushes by.)

Scene Six

(And now we see **MICHEL** *at the end of the sleeping corridor. He is trying to work with the train's two-way radio, a clunky old-fashioned piece of machinery subject to problems.)*

(First we hear the whining screech of the radio trying to find a signal – Oweeeee, Oweeee! – then the crackle of the static when the signal is found.)

MICHEL. Orient Express to Belgrade Station. Orient Express to Belgrade Station. Emergency call number 867. Alert Code Blue. This is important. Do you read me? Hello? Are you there, Belgrade?

RADIO. *(With much static.)* We read you, Express. Pray continue.

MICHEL. We've just left Sofia and the snow is becoming heavier by the minute. I am getting concerned as we head into the mountains. Please prepare your rescue equipment in case of stoppage. Hello? Do you read me?

(Oweeeeeeeee!)

Belgrade?

(Oweeeeeeeee!)

Belgrade, can you hear me?!

Scene Seven

(Lights up on the observation deck. **MARY** *rushes in and looks around. A moment later,* **ARBUTHNOT** *enters.)*

MARY. Oh thank God! I thought you weren't coming!

ARBUTHNOT. What's the matter? I got your note.

MARY. I'll tell you what the matter is! I'm frightened because we shouldn't be doing this!

ARBUTHNOT. Now calm down.

MARY. I can't calm down! We have to stop this!

ARBUTHNOT. Now that's ridiculous.

MARY. No it isn't! Oh that's the trouble with you military men, you never show any *real* emotion, it's always stiff upper lip no matter *what's* going on!

ARBUTHNOT. Mary, we're doing nothing wrong! You have to remember that.

MARY. I'm trying! I really am!

(She hugs **ARBUTHNOT.***)*

ARBUTHNOT. Better?

MARY. Yes, I think so.

ARBUTHNOT. There was a hill near my home in Scotland, and I'd sit for hours watching the trains go by in the valley below. I knew they were heading to exotic locales and I wanted to climb aboard in the worst way.

MARY. But you didn't.

ARBUTHNOT. No. I suppose I knew somehow that I'd break my mother's heart.

MARY. You're a very good man.

ARBUTHNOT. She was a very good woman.

MARY. Do you know what the worst of it is with all this traveling we've been doing? We don't get any privacy. It's just so maddening!

ARBUTHNOT. Well, I don't see anyone around at the moment, do you?

MARY. No, I suppose I don't.

> (**ARBUTHNOT** *takes her in his arms and kisses her with passion. They really go at it. She responds in kind.*)

Oh, James!

ARBUTHNOT. Be strong.

MARY. I will. I promise.

> (*They hear someone coming and spring apart.*)

> (**MACQUEEN** *enters.*)

MACQUEEN. Hi, I-I hope I'm not interrupting.

ARBUTHNOT. Of course you're interrupting, you moron. Are you blind?

MACQUEEN. Oh, I'm sorry! I-I-I can go get a snack or a –

> (*The train stops. They all look up in surprise.*)

ARBUTHNOT. Oh my God, the train is stopping.

MARY. What is it?! What's happening!

MACQUEEN. The snow! Look!

ARBUTHNOT. Oh, not now!

MARY. We've hit a snowdrift!!

ARBUTHNOT. Oh Christ, that's all we need!

MACQUEEN. Shall I go take a look?!

ARBUTHNOT. What good will that do?

MARY. James. He's right. Let him go.

ARBUTHNOT. Mary?

MARY. Go ahead, Mr. MacQueen, we'll be here waiting for you.

MACQUEEN. I'll-I'll be back in a minute!

> (*He runs off.*)

ARBUTHNOT. Why did you send him off like that?

> (**MARY** *takes him in her arms and goes back to kissing him.*)

Scene Eight

(Lights up on **MRS. HUBBARD** *in her compartment, screaming for help.)*

MRS. HUBBARD. Help! Someone come quickly! Help!

*(***BOUC*** *runs in.)*

BOUC. Mrs. Hubbard. What? What is it?!

MRS. HUBBARD. There was a man in my room! He ran off! I'm sure of it!

BOUC. Which way did he go?!

MRS. HUBBARD. *That* way! Just this second!

BOUC. But *madame*, that is where I am coming from and I saw no one.

MRS. HUBBARD. Well... Well maybe he ducked into one of the compartments or something! I don't know. I tell you I was lying there in my bed, dead to the world, and I open my eyes, and I see this man going out the door. And he's wearing a uniform.

BOUC. But where would he come from?

MRS. HUBBARD. I don't know. He just suddenly appeared.

BOUC. And he looked like...?

MRS. HUBBARD. *I don't know! I could barely see him!* One second he was there and then he was gone. He was like a phantom!

BOUC. But how is this possible?

MRS. HUBBARD. HOW SHOULD I KNOW!

BOUC. Perhaps you were dreaming.

MRS. HUBBARD. I wasn't dreaming. I know when I'm dreaming. My mouth gets dry. Does my mouth look dry to you?

BOUC. And your door was locked?

MRS. HUBBARD. Of course it was locked, but people have keys, don't they? I'll bet you have keys. Don't you own the company?

BOUC. No, *madame*, I *run* the company. And I will look into it.

MRS. HUBBARD. Well, all right then. But hurry up about it. I don't feel safe!

(*MRS. HUBBARD closes her door. POIROT puts his head out of his room.*)

POIROT. She is keeping you busy, our Mrs. Hubbard.

BOUC. You have no idea. She insists that there was a man inside her compartment.

POIROT. Michel perhaps?

BOUC. Impossible. He is helping my engineer at the moment.

(*POIROT cocks his head. Something is wrong.*)

POIROT. *Attends.* We are not moving.

BOUC. You are telling me.

POIROT. A snowdrift?

BOUC. *Oui.* And we are stuck until men are sent from Belgrade to dig us out.

POIROT. *Ah non, non, non, non, non, non, non.*

BOUC. I am sorry, my friend. But I promise, you will be completely comfortable for as long as it takes.

(*MRS. HUBBARD puts her head out her door.*)

MRS. HUBBARD. Bouc! Have you tracked him down yet?!

BOUC. Not yet, *madame.*

MRS. HUBBARD. Well keep trying!

BOUC. (*To POIROT.*) Goodnight, my friend. I hope you get a good sleep tonight, because that will make one of us.

MRS. HUBBARD. And hurry up about it!

(*BOUC walks away. POIROT retreats into his compartment and looks at his watch.*)

POIROT. I wonder...

(*Immediately we hear the mischievous passage from Rossini's overture to* La Gazza Ladra *that begins approximately two minutes in.*)

Scene Nine

(The night fades to morning and we are still in the corridor. The **PRINCESS** *is making her way to the dining car and sees* **GRETA** *ahead of her.)*

PRINCESS. Greta! It is I! Slow down!

GRETA. Oh good morning, princess. *(To* **MACQUEEN**.*)* Good morning!

*(***MACQUEEN** *comes by with a breakfast tray and they have to squeeze past each other.)*

MACQUEEN. *(To* **PRINCESS**.*)* Good morning.

PRINCESS. *(To* **MACQUEEN**.*)* Good morning!

MACQUEEN. *(To* **GRETA**.*)* Good morning.

GRETA. *(To* **MACQUEEN**.*)* Good morning.

*(***MACQUEEN** *steps in the* **PRINCESS**'*s way.)*

MACQUEEN. My fault! Good morning.

(Knocking.)

Mr. Ratchett?

(Knock, knock, knock.)

Sir?

(Knock, knock, knock.)

Sir, could you open the door, please?

(Sensing that something is wrong.)

Hello?!

*(***BOUC** *and* **POIROT** *enter.)*

BOUC. Is something wrong?

MACQUEEN. He isn't answering.

(He tries the door.)

And it's locked.

BOUC. *Monsieur* Ratchett, are you all right?

POIROT. The pass key, perhaps.

BOUC. Of course.

GRETA. I hope he is not being ill.

PRINCESS. Shh.

BOUC. There's a chain.

MACQUEEN. Hello?

POIROT. You must force the door.

BOUC. It will break and need repairing.

POIROT. Quickly! Do you not feel the air from the room? It is freezing. Quickly!

GRETA. *(Wailing.)* I do not like this at all!

> *(Bang! The three men break open the door with a crash. As they enter the room, it opens out so we, the audience, are in the room with them.)*
>
> *(Sitting up in bed is* **SAMUEL RATCHETT***, the chest of his pajamas crimson with blood. He looks garish and hideous.)*
>
> *(Screeeeeeeeeeeeech!! There is a sound of terror in the score – then* **GRETA** *screams and falls to her knees.)*

Eeeee! Dear God, dear God, it is awful!

MACQUEEN. Mr. Ratchett!

GRETA. I cannot look!

MACQUEEN. Do you see his chest?!

PRINCESS. It is horrible!

BOUC. *(Reaching to touch* **RATCHETT***'s chest.)* I cannot believe it!

POIROT. *Do not touch anything! Not a speck!*

GRETA. *(Hysterical.)* IT IS HUMAN LIFE! IT IS WRONG!

PRINCESS. Greta, calm down!

POIROT. Princess, could you escort Miss Ohlsson to her room, please.

PRINCESS. Come along, Greta.

> *(***GRETA** *wails with distress and the two women exit.)*

MACQUEEN. Holy cow.

BOUC. There has never been such a thing in the history of my company!

> (**POIROT** *removes a pair of tweezers from his pocket and delicately moves the pajamas away from the wounds.*)

What are you doing?

POIROT. I am examining the wounds – there appear to be seven – no, eight stab wounds to the chest. *Monsieur* MacQueen, when did you see him last?

MACQUEEN. *Me?* I-I-I don't know anything! He was fine last night when I put out his wine.

POIROT. You are his secretary. What do you know about him?

MACQUEEN. Not very much. He-he-he-he never spoke about himself at all. Frankly, I think he was hiding something. That's just an impression.

POIROT. And why was that do you think?

MACQUEEN. I-I think he was fleeing from America to get away from something, and I think he managed it until a few weeks ago.

POIROT. And then?

MACQUEEN. He began to get some threatening letters. They're in my room. Do you want to see them?

POIROT. Yes. Go quickly. And please ask the countess to join me here.

MACQUEEN. I'll be right back!

> (**MACQUEEN** *runs off.*)

BOUC. It is incredible for such a thing to happen on *my train*! Ooh, it's freezing in here.

POIROT. You have observed the window.

BOUC. *Oui*, it is open.

POIROT. And what do you see outside?

BOUC. Nothing.

POIROT. Exactly. No footprints. No marks in the snow. Which means that no one entered or left through the window.

BOUC. Then why is it open?

POIROT. I assume to mislead the police when they arrive.

BOUC. The police?!

POIROT. Of course the police. It is murder.

BOUC. The Yugoslavian police department? Oh no, no, no, no, no, no, no. We do not want them. You must solve the murder, then *you* tell *them* who did it.

POIROT. I have interfered too much already.

BOUC. But my company is at stake!

POIROT. But *mon ami* –

BOUC. Just think what a Yugoslavian police inquiry would do to my company. People would say, "Oh no, I cannot travel on the Orient Express, I could be murdered in my bed," and our sales would suffer and I would lose my *clients*!

POIROT. But I am due in London in three days' time.

BOUC. Then solve it in two! You are a magician. I have seen you work! You listen, you look, you pester, you make yourself a pain in the backside, then suddenly poof!, the case is solved like *that*!

POIROT. The police would be angry.

BOUC. The Yugoslavian police department? They are like the three stooges in the movie house. They poke each other in the eyes by accident. They would be thrilled not to have to do any work. If you save them the job, they will put up a statue of you in the center of Zagreb!

POIROT. I would need a plan of the coach.

BOUC. Done.

POIROT. And the passports and tickets of everyone on board.

BOUC. Done.

(The **COUNTESS** *arrives.)*

COUNTESS. Excuse me, but you have asked to see me – *oh dear God.*

POIROT. Forgive me, countess, but I understand you were trained as a physician, so I thought perhaps you could help me with the body.

COUNTESS. I am happy to help.

> *(Without hesitation, she strips off her jacket and rolls up her sleeves.)*

POIROT. I'm afraid it is not a very pleasant sight.

COUNTESS. I have seen worse, believe me. I volunteered in the war.

> *(The* **COUNTESS** *begins examining the body.)*

POIROT. *Regardes.* The left side of his face is slightly red, do you see?

COUNTESS. I do. It has been slapped.

BOUC. How do you know?

COUNTESS. Because I slapped it. I count eight separate wounds.

POIROT. That was my count also. Can you estimate the time of death?

COUNTESS. I would say it is between eight and ten hours ago, which puts the time between midnight and two o'clock.

POIROT. I am in accord.

COUNTESS. It appears that the killer was wild – in a frenzy of some sort.

POIROT. *Regardes.* See this. Of the eight stab wounds, five appear strong and three are mere scratches. And wait, do you see, the wounds are from different directions. Do you see it? I need a pencil.

BOUC. Here.

POIROT. *Bon.* Now watch. We place the pencil inside each wound and push it gently...

BOUC. Ugh! Is this necessary?

COUNTESS. Perhaps the man changed hands during the stabbing.

BOUC. Or there were two assailants. One right-handed and one left-handed.

COUNTESS. One strong, one weak.

POIROT. It is not impossible. But now another question presents itself: why did Mr. Ratchett not fight back when all the while he had this gun under his pillow?

> (**POIROT** *pulls the revolver out from under the pillow.*)

COUNTESS. *Oh là là.*

BOUC. *Alors.* May I see it?

> (**BOUC** *takes the gun.*)

COUNTESS. How did you find it?

POIROT. He showed it to me yesterday so I knew it was here somewhere.

BOUC. It is an automatic and I believe it is loaded.

> (*He waves it around.*)

POIROT. *Attention!*

COUNTESS. *Ah!*

BOUC. Wait! There is a safety switch, it is not on.

POIROT. *S'il vous plaît, mon ami!* Have you not heard of the fatal accident?!

> (*He takes the gun from* **BOUC,** *but stops suddenly and sniffs the air.*)

Un moment.

> (*He sniffs again and puts his finger up.*)

I have a very good nose.

> (*He picks up* **RATCHETT***'s empty wine glass and sniffs.*)

Aha. Smell the glass of wine.

COUNTESS. It smells of almonds.

*(She pulls **RATCHETT**'s eyelids up and examines his eyes.)*

COUNTESS. He was clearly drugged, which is why –

POIROT & COUNTESS. He did not fight back.

POIROT. Puh, puh. What is this in his pocket? *Voilà.*

*(He pulls a pocket watch from **RATCHETT**'s pajama pocket.)*

BOUC. It is a watch, and the face is smashed!

COUNTESS. It is stopped at 1:15.

BOUC. Haha! At last! We have something important, yes?! It is the time of death, and the countess said between midnight and two! So there it is! It could not be clearer! 1:15 is the time of death, it is obvious.

POIROT. It is possible.

BOUC. What do you mean it is possible? What is wrong with it?

POIROT. I do not know yet what is wrong and what is right because *I am still investigating*! Here is a pipe cleaner, and here is a match, and here is another match of a different shape. There are dozens of clues in this room and it makes me suspicious!

BOUC. Look at this, on the floor.

COUNTESS. *(Picking it up.)* It is a lady's handkerchief with the letter H on it.

POIROT. Yet another clue. And who is H? Eh? As in *Hamlet* –

COUNTESS. "That is the question." There is Mrs. Hubbard, and I believe that her first name is Helen.

POIROT. And the princess?

BOUC. Her name is Natalya Dragomiroff. And there is Mary Debenham and Greta Ohlsson and James Arbuthnot and Hector MacQueen and I am Constantine Bouc, and such a thing like this has never happened in the history of the Wagon-Lit and it will ruin my company *and I want you to solve it immediately*!

POIROT. You are upset.

BOUC. *I am very upset! A man has been murdered on my train!*

POIROT. It will be all right.

BOUC. *I hope so!* I will smoke a cigarette.

POIROT. That is a good idea.

BOUC. And oh my God, just look at this ashtray. My people are lying down on the job.

> *(He picks up the ashtray and is about to empty it.)*

POIROT. NO! STOP!

> *(**BOUC** has frozen in place. **POIROT** gazes at the contents of the ashtray, then brings out a pair of tweezers.)*

Do you not see? There is a piece of paper that has been burned, perhaps to hide its contents.

> *(He peers at it.)*

There seems to be something written on it. What I need right now is a lady's hat box. Countess, do you keep such a thing?

COUNTESS. Of course I do.

> *(She hurries away.)*

POIROT. I greatly admire that creature, Bouc. Did you see? She did not ask me a single question. I ask for a hat box, she gets me a hat box. I ask her for help with the body, she rolls up her sleeves. Suddenly I desire to be young again. Do not move.

> *(He rushes into his own room, calling behind him.)*

I am getting a spirit lamp! I use it to heat the wax for my moustache.

BOUC. And why do you need a spirit lamp?

POIROT. *(Calling.)* Because this time I am using science to catch the guilty party. Usually for me it is the psychology – the mind of the killer – but not with these clues.

BOUC. Why not?

POIROT. *(Still calling.)* Because I do not trust them! *(Running back into the room with the lamp.)* The handkerchief: did a woman drop it or did a man put it there and say, "I will make this look like a woman's crime." The same thing with the pipe cleaner, *eh*? "I will make it look like a *man* has done it." There is also the watch, the gun, the window, the match, the wine – there are too many clues *and I am unhappy*!

    (The **COUNTESS** *enters.)*

COUNTESS. Your hat box, *monsieur*.

POIROT. *Merci, madame.*

COUNTESS. *Je vous en pris.*

POIROT. If I asked you to leave your husband and come away with me to Monte Carlo, what would you say?

COUNTESS. I would say give me five minutes, I need to pack.

POIROT. I will get back to you. In the meantime, please hold this, thank you.

    *(***POIROT** *opens the box and hands the hat to the* **COUNTESS***, then removes two humps of wire netting from the box and hands them to* **BOUC***. Then he lights his spirit lamp. He then places one of the humps of netting beside the lamp, then carefully puts the shred of paper on top of that, then puts the other hump of netting over the first.)*

Excellent. I believe that this paper is the remains of a note, perhaps a threat, that was burned to conceal the information it contained. Now I want you to watch very closely, for I believe that some letters will appear, *but only briefly* as the flame is striking them, and we must regard them while we can. Now let us put it over the flame like so...

(He places the contraption over the flame and suddenly a few letters glow for a moment on the paper; we see them on a projection across the set:

Remember little Daisy Armstrong.

Then whoosh!, they're gone in a burning blackness.)

POIROT. Haha! Did you see it?!

BOUC. "Remember little Daisy Armstrong."

COUNTESS. But what does it mean?

BOUC. There was a case in America three years ago.

POIROT. Four.

BOUC. A little girl was murdered, it was in all the papers.

COUNTESS. I do not remember.

POIROT. It was a case most horrible.

BOUC. Horrible.

POIROT. A young girl named Daisy Armstrong was kidnapped from her home in Long Island, New York.

DAISY'S VOICE. *Mama! Daddy!*

POIROT. The ransom was set at two hundred thousand dollars and it was paid –

BOUC. But Daisy was not returned to her parents.

POIROT. Three days later, they found the little girl – dead, murdered – in the woods not far away from her home.

MOTHER'S VOICE. *(Offstage.)* Nooooooooo!

POIROT. The police caught the man who did it but he had ties to organized crime and they got him off by changing the evidence. He would have been lynched if he had been found by the public, but he gave them the slip and disappeared.

COUNTESS. But what has this got to do with Ratchett?

POIROT. I think we can guess this, no?

BOUC. Of course!

POIROT. Mr. MacQueen said that Ratchett was fleeing from something in America and that he succeeded until the letters began arriving.

COUNTESS. Then you think –?

POIROT. That Ratchett's real name was Bruno Cassetti, the man who murdered little Daisy Armstrong.

COUNTESS. Good God.

(**MACQUEEN** *enters.*)

MACQUEEN. Excuse me. Mr. Poirot, I found the letters.

POIROT. *Bon. Merci.* And so it begins. Monsieur Bouc, please gather the passports of everyone in the carriage, then send to me the princess and Miss Ohlsson together, then Mr. MacQueen, then Mrs. Hubbard. Now *vite, vite,* before the trail is cold! It is clear that someone on this train committed this murder, and I will find out who it is, I promise you!

(*Blackout. We hear more of the wild ride, discordant sounds of Rossini's overture to* La Gazza Ladra.)

Scene Ten

(Bang! The lights come up instantly on the dining car. **POIROT, BOUC,** *the* **PRINCESS,** *and* **GRETA.***)*

PRINCESS. *Monsieur* Poirot, we are here out of a sense of duty, that is all. I do not like having my day disturbed.

POIROT. Then let us begin immediately. Now it says in your passport that you are Russian.

PRINCESS. That is correct. I have been in exile since the Bolshevik dogs took over.

POIROT. And I see that your first name is –

PRINCESS. Natalya.

POIROT. And is this your handkerchief, *madame*?

PRINCESS. Of course not. It has the letter *H* on it. My initials are N. D. Natalya Dragomiroff.

POIROT. Is it yours, *mademoiselle*?

GRETA. No, no, I could not afford such a beautiful thing as this. It would be a sin.

PRINCESS. Oh!

POIROT. And may I ask each of you where you were last night between midnight and two o'clock.

PRINCESS. I could not sleep, so at midnight the Countess Andrenyi and I read a book together in my room. Out loud. It is the very best way to get to sleep when you are anxious.

POIROT. And what were you anxious about?

PRINCESS. The Bolsheviks.

POIROT. And what book did you read?

PRINCESS. *A Tale of Two Cities*, it is very comforting.

POIROT. And you, Miss Ohlsson? Where were you?

GRETA. I was in my room with Miss Debenham, who is also nice. We talked from twelve o'clock until two o'clock and then we slept. You can ask her!

POIROT. And have either of you ever been to America?

PRINCESS. Yes, many times.

GRETA. I have not been to America but I must go some day to raise money for my babies in Africa.

POIROT. You are very religious.

GRETA. *Ja*, since I was little girl and Jaysus came to visit me in my garden. He spoke vith me, und told me I must verk hard to help little babies in Africa.

POIROT. And I'm sure you have done it beautifully, *mademoiselle*. Just one more question for both of you ladies. Are you aware of the identity of the man who was killed last night?

GRETA. His name was Ratchett.

> *(Sob.)*

And I pray for his soul.

PRINCESS. No, my dear, his name was Bruno Cassetti, the countess told me, and what *I* pray is that his soul is damned and that he burns in hell for all eternity.

GRETA. Princess!

PRINCESS. He murdered a girl named Daisy Armstrong and her grandmother is my dearest friend. You would know her as the actress Linda Arden.

BOUC. She was very great.

PRINCESS. Not *was, monsieur*. She *is* very great. She is very much alive and remains the greatest actress of the American stage. And when her five year old granddaughter was murdered by this *monster* Cassetti, it took her years to recover, indeed she has not *yet* recovered!

POIROT. There were four who died?

PRINCESS. No, *five*, monsieur! *Five* people died! Little Daisy, and then her mother, who was pregnant, died in childbirth, and the baby died, too. And the little girl's father, Colonel Armstrong, could not live with what happened and ended his life! And a housemaid as well! Five human souls were extinguished. So please forgive me, Greta, if I take the view that there is no forgiveness in a case such as this and that Mr. Cassetti should have been *flogged to death and his remains cut up and thrown onto a rubbish heap*!!

GRETA. *(Crying out.) Ahh!*

> *(**GRETA** runs from the room. The **PRINCESS** runs after her and bumps into **MACQUEEN**, who is just entering.)*

PRINCESS. Greta, please! Greta!

MACQUEEN. I'm-I'm-I'm so sorry.

> *(The **PRINCESS** is gone.)*

POIROT. *Monsieur* MacQueen, please sit down.

MACQUEEN. Of-of-of course. Are they all right?

POIROT. They will be fine, I assure you. Now tell me, please, what exactly were your duties as secretary to your employer?

MACQUEEN. Well I-I wrote his letters and did his errands and things.

POIROT. And you knew him only as Samuel Ratchett.

MACQUEEN. How else would I know him?

POIROT. His real name was Bruno Cassetti.

MACQUEEN. Holy God. Are you sure of that?

BOUC. Then you know about the Armstrong case?

MACQUEEN. You bet I do. My father was the district attorney for the state of New York and he brought the case against that...son of a bitch. I'm sorry, but you have no idea what he did to that family. And they were so kind to me!

POIROT. Can you tell us who was in the Armstrong household?

MACQUEEN. Mrs. Armstrong had a sister. She went to graduate school, but after the tragedy she moved to Europe and I think she got married. Her name was *Hel*ena. And also Mrs. Armstrong's mother would come to visit. She was an actress.

POIROT. Anyone else?

MACQUEEN. There was a governess and a baby nurse, and then poor Suzanne. She was a French housemaid – she came from Paris – and my father's office thought she might be implicated, and...and she was so distraught from the accusations that she –

BOUC. Killed herself.

MACQUEEN. *(Nods.)* Only it turned out that she was innocent. My father was shattered. He never recovered.

POIROT. And where were you last night between midnight and two o'clock?

MACQUEEN. Twelve to two? I-I was with Colonel Arbuthnot on the observation deck.

POIROT. And did you see anyone last night you did not recognize?

MACQUEEN. No. I saw Michel the conductor, and the other conductor, and Colonel Arbuthnot, and Miss Debenham –

BOUC. The "other conductor"?

POIROT. There is a second conductor?

MACQUEEN. I guess so. I saw him.

BOUC. He was in uniform?

MACQUEEN. Yeah. The same one that Michel wears.

BOUC. And what did he look like?

MACQUEEN. I don't know. He had his hat pulled down. He was small-boned, you know what I mean? Sort of feminine.

POIROT. Did you speak with him?

MACQUEEN. I said hello and he just kept going.

POIROT. You are very helpful, thank you. You may go. And please ask Michel to come see me.

MACQUEEN. Sure thing. I'll see you later.

(As soon as **MACQUEEN** *exits,* **BOUC** *cries out.)*

BOUC. Haha! I knew we would get a breakthrough! Mrs. Hubbard was telling the truth, I should have listened. The murderer wore a uniform, and the question now is where did he go!

POIROT. No, no, my friend, the question now is whether such a man exists. He could be an invention of *Monsieur* MacQueen.

BOUC. But why would he lie? He is not the murderer.

POIROT. Why not?

BOUC. Because he is not the type! It is a crime of passion by someone Italian or Hungarian! A man with blood in his veins!

POIROT. I have now looked at all of the passports and there is one that troubles me. There is a grease spot on the signature page and it obscures the first letter of the Christian name and I believe it is telling.

BOUC. Who is it?!

MRS. HUBBARD. *(At the door.)* Knock, knock. Excuse me but I need to talk to you.

BOUC. If you could please wait your turn –

MRS. HUBBARD. No, I cannot wait my turn because you owe me an *apology.*

BOUC. I do?

MRS. HUBBARD. You thought I was crazy.

BOUC. *Pardon, madame,* I do not know to what you are referring –

MRS. HUBBARD. To what I am referring is the man in my room last night! You didn't believe me, but guess what, I have a surprise for you. There *was* a man and I can prove it! He left a *button! Look!*

> *(She pulls out a brass button and* **BOUC** *peers at it.)*

BOUC. It says "Orient Express."

MRS. HUBBARD. It sure as heck does, and it's just like the ones that Michel wears on *his* uniform.

POIROT. *(Examining it.)* And you found it...?

MRS. HUBBARD. On the floor this morning, bright as you please – next to my big toe after I put these tootsies down on the floor when I woke up.

POIROT. And you waited until now to tell us?

MRS. HUBBARD. I just woke up! It's called a vacation! And I just heard about Ratchett's murder and I thought that maybe this button guy did it. Ya see it all adds up. He goes into Ratchett's room, kills him, comes out through my room, I wake up at, like, 1:15 and see him – well, not see him exactly, I sort of feel his presence – and do you realize *he could have strangled me in my bed, or shot me or something*!

POIROT. The dead man's name was not Ratchett, *madame*, it was Bruno Cassetti. Does that mean anything to you?

MRS. HUBBARD. No.

POIROT. Have you ever heard of the Armstrong case?

MRS. HUBBARD. You mean that poor kid who got murdered? It was national news. The whole world knew about it. So what?

POIROT. May I ask where you were last night between midnight and two o'clock?

MRS. HUBBARD. Oh, great, so now I'm a suspect? You know you should read some detective stories and get some tips.

POIROT. Twelve to two, *madame*.

MRS. HUBBARD. I just told you! I was alone in bed around one o'clock and then a few minutes later some man walks into my room and scares the living bejesus out of me.

POIROT. Mrs. Hubbard, would you write your signature on this paper, please?

MRS. HUBBARD. I beg your pardon?

POIROT. Your signature, so I can see your handwriting.

MRS. HUBBARD. *(Writing.)* I always thought the French were screwy.

BOUC. He is from Belgium.

MRS. HUBBARD. Exactly.

(*As which moment,* **ARBUTHNOT** *bursts into the room.*)

ARBUTHNOT. Sorry to interrupt, but I'm looking for Miss Debenham.

POIROT. She is not here.

BOUC. Did you try her room?

ARBUTHNOT. I tried everywhere I can think of and she's gone!

BOUC. Have you tried the carriages at the back of the train?

ARBUTHNOT. Of course I did. I got Michel to open the doors and she wasn't in any of them.

BOUC. Well she cannot be far, *monsieur.* It is a very small train.

ARBUTHNOT. You don't understand what I'm saying, *monsieur.* There was a murder on this train last night and that has certain *implications, does it not*?!

(*Suddenly we hear a terrible scream, followed by a gunshot.*)

MARY. (*Offstage.*) EEEEEEEE!

(*Bang!*)

ARBUTHNOT. Oh my God! It's her!

BOUC. What happened?!

POIROT. *Quickly! This way!*

(*They run out of the room and we follow them into the corridor. Lights flash this way and that as though we are somehow in the minds of the pursuers.*)

ARBUTHNOT. Where did it come from?!

BOUC. I couldn't tell!

MRS. HUBBARD. What's going on?!

ARBUTHNOT. Mary?!

BOUC. Miss Debenham?!

GRETA. Oh dear God!

MACQUEEN. *(Joining them.)* What's happening?!

COUNTESS. *(Joining them.)* I heard a gunshot!

ARBUTHNOT. She's not in here!

MACQUEEN. Try Ratchett's room!

ARBUTHNOT. Mary!!

PRINCESS. Miss Debenham?!

BOUC. Push!

COUNTESS. Push hard!

MICHEL. I'm trying!

ARBUTHNOT. God almighty!

> *(**GRETA** screams.)*

> *(Bang! The door flies open and they all burst into **RATCHETT**'s room.)*

> *(**MARY** is lying on the floor in a pool of blood, with **RATCHETT**'s gun nearby on the floor.)*

> *(We hear a screech of sound.)*

> *(Blackout!)*

ACT II

Scene One

(A blast of discordant sound is heard: The opening bars of the "Stüermisch Bewegt" from Mahler's Fifth Symphony. *The lights come up and we're exactly where we were at the close of Act I. Everyone is frozen, staring at* **MARY** *on the floor in a pool of blood with the gun beside her.)*

POIROT. *TOUCH NOTHING!* Countess.

COUNTESS. Of course.

> *(The* **COUNTESS** *hurries to* **MARY** *and kneels and begins to minister to her.)*

She's still alive.

BOUC. Oh thank God!

> *(***MARY** *stirs and moans.)*

ARBUTHNOT. Mary!

MARY. What...what happened?

ARBUTHNOT. You were shot, for God's sake!

COUNTESS. I need my medical bag.

MRS. HUBBARD. I'll get it!

COUNTESS. Quickly! Compartment twelve!

POIROT. Michel, please search the train.

MICHEL. *Oui, monsieur.*

BOUC. I'll go with him.

MACQUEEN. Me, too!

POIROT. Wait! Do you have a gun?

MICHEL. There is one for emergencies in the porter's box.

POIROT. Take it with you. This is not a game.

MICHEL. Yes sir.

BOUC. Come quickly.

> (*BOUC,* **MICHEL,** *and* **MACQUEEN** *run off, as* **MRS. HUBBARD** *returns with the first aid kit.*)

COUNTESS. Can you sit upright?

MARY. I-I think so. Ow!

PRINCESS. There is a great deal of blood. I do not like blood.

MRS. HUBBARD. Nobody likes blood. Here's the kit.

COUNTESS. Thank you. It is only your arm?

MARY. Yes.

COUNTESS. You have not been hurt elsewhere?

MARY. No.

> (*The* **COUNTESS** *removes a pair of scissors.*)

COUNTESS. Do not be alarmed. I am merely cutting the sleeve of your blouse so I can have a better look.

> (*The* **COUNTESS** *cuts the sleeve of the blouse up the side and then off, exposing* **MARY***'s bloody arm. Everyone winces.*)

GRETA. I cannot watch.

COUNTESS. This may hurt a bit. It is...what do you call it in English. *Jód* –

POIROT. *Iodine.**

MRS. HUBBARD. Iodine.

MARY. *OW!*

ARBUTHNOT. Be careful, will you!

MARY. I'm all right, colonel.

COUNTESS. You are remarkably fortunate, Miss Debenham. Two inches to the left and it would have been fatal.

ARBUTHNOT. Well, thank God for small blessings!

POIROT. Countess, may I ask Miss Debenham a question?

COUNTESS. Are you well enough?

---

*Pronounces it as in French, "Ee-o-deen."

MARY. I-I think so.

POIROT. It is very simple, *mademoiselle*: who shot you?

MARY. I... I don't know. I-I only caught a glimpse of him. He was –

POIROT. What?

PRINCESS. Tell us.

MARY. It makes no sense. He was in a kind of uniform. But I may have imagined it.

POIROT. Can you tell us what happened?

(*During the following, the* **COUNTESS** *continues to clean and bandage the wound.*)

MARY. I'll try. I-I woke up this morning feeling disoriented, as though I'd been drugged or something, and I had this splitting headache. So I looked through my suitcase for some aspirin, but I didn't have any. So then I stumbled out of the room and I saw that Mrs. Hubbard's door was ajar. I called to her but she wasn't there and then – I know I shouldn't have – but I went into her room. (*To* **MRS. HUBBARD.**) I'm sorry.

MRS. HUBBARD. That's quite all right.

POIROT. Go on.

MARY. My head was splitting open by this time and I wasn't thinking straight – so I looked for some aspirin in Mrs. Hubbard's makeup bag. And there was this *knife* and it was covered with *blood*!

GRETA. A knife!

MRS. HUBBARD. In my bag?

MARY. Yes.

POIROT. Where is it?

MARY. I left it where it was. I felt *so frightened.*

MRS. HUBBARD. Holy cow. I'll go get it –!

POIROT. *STOP!* You will *not* "go get it." I will retrieve it, when I am ready. Now Miss Debenham, continue.

MRS. HUBBARD. Well, let me just say that this does prove there was a man was in my room last night, like I was –

POIROT. Mrs. Hubbard!

MRS. HUBBARD. Sorry.

PRINCESS. You talk too much.

MRS. HUBBARD. I beg your pardon.

POIROT. Miss Debenham.

MARY. Well, I was frightened when I saw the knife and I must have backed into Mr. Ratchett's room, and then I turned and saw the body on the bed with all the blood and the wounds, and I – I screamed, and then I saw the man and the gun and that's all I remember!

> *(She starts to cry.)*

COUNTESS. *(Comforting MARY.)* It's all right.

POIROT. Are you sure it was a man?

MARY. I *think* so. I assumed it was. I suppose I'm not positive.

PRINCESS. He must have been hiding in this room behind the door, waiting to escape.

MRS. HUBBARD. So if I'd come in here first, then *whammo!* No more show tunes in the shower.

PRINCESS. And that would have been a terrible loss.

POIROT. Mrs. Hubbard, can you tell me where you keep your makeup bag?

MRS. HUBBARD. Gladly. Right behind the door, hanging on the handle.

> *(**POIROT** goes to get it.)*

If these compartments were bigger, I wouldn't have to hang my makeup bag on a door handle like some drama school kid in a Rudolf Friml operetta living out of a hold-all and *holy God!*

> *(**POIROT** has retrieved the makeup bag from which he has extracted a vicious looking dagger covered with blood and **MRS. HUBBARD** has just seen it.)*

GRETA. *(Grabbing the **PRINCESS**.)* I cannot look!

ARBUTHNOT. *(Reaching for it.)* I've never seen one like that before.

POIROT. Ah, ah. I will be analyzing it for fingerprints. In the meantime, will you all please leave and do not touch *anything* as you go. When I have finished in here, I will be in the dining car and I would like to see Miss Debenham –

ARBUTHNOT. Now see here!

POIROT. *If she is able.* Then Mrs. Hubbard, and then Miss Ohlsson and the princess again.

PRINCESS. Me?!

POIROT. Countess, will you be so kind as to escort Miss Debenham to her room, please.

COUNTESS. Of course. You are strong enough?

MARY. I'm much better. Thank you.

ARBUTHNOT. *(To* **POIROT**, *angry.)* I see no reason to put Miss Debenham through anything stressful at the moment, and I suggest you *don't.*

POIROT. I will bear that in mind.

(Everyone starts to leave.)

PRINCESS. I hope you solve all this quickly, *monsieur.* I am not afraid of dying, but I would rather not speed up the process.

MRS. HUBBARD. I intend to sue this company on the grounds of sheer anxiety.

(Everyone leaves except **POIROT**, *and we hear the thoughtful opening of the first movement of Bach's* Cello Suite No. 2 In D Minor.*)*

POIROT. *Eh bien, madame,* you are not the only one who is anxious at the moment.

(Fade into the following scene.)

Scene Two

(The end of the corridor. **MICHEL** *is on the two-way radio. "Oweeeee!")*

MICHEL. Zagreb, come in, please. We have an emergency!

(Radio sounds: high pitched screeches and static.)

We cannot reach Belgrade, and we are twenty miles from the nearest town. We need assistance!

(Radio sounds.)

Zagreb, come in!

Scene Three

(We shift to the dining car where **POIROT** *is waiting, as* **BOUC** *bursts suddenly into the room.)*

BOUC. No one! There is no one, I tell you! Not a single person is on this train who should not be here!

POIROT. You are positive?

BOUC. *Entirely!* It has gone too far. *Our lives are in danger!*

POIROT. It is like a magic trick.

BOUC. It is unbelievable! I told Michel to go on searching and he may find *something.*

POIROT. I do not expect so.

BOUC. Then where did he go, this man who is dressed like a train conductor?

POIROT. I have no idea! That is the problem! Every time I find a piece of the puzzle, there is a suspect who has an alibi. Colonel Arbuthnot? He could have a grudge against Cassetti from a business dealing – but then MacQueen gives him an alibi from twelve to two, they are chatting on the observation deck! Aha, I say. What about Miss Ohlssohn? – she is strange, there is something not right about her – but she swears that she and Miss Debenham are up all night *chattering* in the room they are sharing. And so it goes with Mrs. Hubbard and the princess *and now Miss Debenham is shot and I am out of suspects*!

*(***ARBUTHNOT** *and* **MARY** *enter.)*

ARBUTHNOT. Poirot! I have brought Miss Debenham as you requested, now what do you want with her?

POIROT. I merely wish to ask her some questions. Colonel, you may go.

ARBUTHNOT. I beg your pardon?

POIROT. You are not needed for this.

ARBUTHNOT. Well, I'm sorry to hear it, because I'm staying.

POIROT. I am sorry also because you are not.

ARBUTHNOT. Now listen to me you little *Frenchman* –

BOUC. He is Belgian.

ARBUTHNOT. I don't care if he's the man in the moon, I'm not leaving her!

MARY. It's all right, James. Honestly. I'm sure it won't take long.

POIROT. She is correct. I need a mere ten minutes.

ARBUTHNOT. Well, I don't like it! Do you understand? And you can put that in your meerschaum pipe and smoke it!

BOUC. That is Sherlock Holmes.

ARBUTHNOT. Oh, go to hell!

(**ARBUTHNOT** *stalks out.*)

POIROT. *Bon.* Please sit down, Miss Debenham. There is much pain?

MARY. Well, it's rather sore, that's all.

POIROT. You are very brave. Let us all be grateful that it is not worse.

BOUC. *(Crossing himself.)* Thank the Lord.

POIROT. Now Miss Debenham. In the hotel yesterday I heard you speaking with the colonel and you said you were terrified you would miss the train. Can you tell me why it was so important to you?

MARY. It wasn't that at all. I didn't want to be late.

POIROT. But you said you wanted to, "Get it over with." Get it, "All behind you." Get what behind you? You seemed quite agitated.

MARY. I'm afraid you're reading into it. I'm tremendously punctual, that's all.

POIROT. Aha. *Pardon.* It is my profession. Sometimes I am too *imaginatif.* And you and the colonel are very close, I take it?

MARY. We only met a few days ago, and I suppose we rather hit it off.

POIROT. And as for the murder, I assume you know that the dead man was Bruno Cassetti.

MARY. I heard.

POIROT. And what do you know of the kidnapping?

MARY. Not much, I'm afraid. I've never been to the States.

POIROT. Aha. I see. And what is it that brought you to Istanbul?

MARY. I lived with a family for about a year. I'm a governess.

POIROT. And can you tell me your whereabouts last night between midnight and two o'clock?

MARY. I was in my room with Miss Ohlsson. We chatted until quite late. You see she...she talks quite a bit, especially when she's anxious, and I may have dozed off for a few minutes.

POIROT. I see.

MARY. May I go?

POIROT. You may. Oh wait. There is one last thing. Would you sign your name please.

MARY. All right.

> *(She does.)*

It's a good thing I'm left-handed. I'd have trouble signing with my right at the moment.

POIROT. *Merci.*

BOUC. Please get some rest. And on behalf of the company I will have some champagne sent straight to your room.

MARY. Thank you so much.

> *(She exits.)*

BOUC. *(Calling to her.)* And if there is anything else I can do to help, please let me know.

> *(Pleasantly.)*

Goodbye! Goodbye!

> *(He closes the door.)*

Oh my God, can you imagine if she had died? Thank goodness she is such a lovely young woman.

POIROT. She is more than lovely. She is a complete liar.

BOUC. *(Incredulous.)* Miss Debenham?

POIROT. She claims that she is not well-acquainted with the colonel, yet they are clearly *intime*. To him she said she wanted to put something behind her and now she pretends that these words mean nothing.

BOUC. But she was shot!

POIROT. In the arm.

BOUC. It could have killed her!

POIROT. I wonder.

BOUC. About what?! *Oh là là,* you do not suspect her of Cassetti's murder –?

POIROT. It is not impossible.

BOUC. But it *is* impossible. She is cool. She is methodical. She would not stab a man to death, she would sue him in court!

POIROT. *Non, non,* you are wrong if you think this crime is sudden and passionate. This is a long-headed crime, *mon ami,* I would stake my career on it. Look at this.

> (**POIROT** *produces the sleeve of* **MARY***'s blouse that was cut off by the* **COUNTESS***.*)

BOUC. The sleeve of her blouse. So what?

POIROT. There is a powder burn at the entry point.

BOUC. Which means?

POIROT. That the gun was very close to the sleeve when it went off.

BOUC. So what? The man was two feet away!

> (**MICHEL** *hurries in.*)

MICHEL. *(At the door.) Pardon, messieurs.* I have finished the search.

BOUC. And, and, and?

MICHEL. Nothing. There is no sign of an intruder anywhere. If you like, I can show you.

POIROT. *Non, non, c'est tout.* Would you now be so kind as to remove your tunic, please?

> (**MICHEL,** *confused, looks to* **BOUC** *for guidance, and* **BOUC** *nods.* **MICHEL** *removes his tunic and hands it to* **POIROT.**)

I see that none of your buttons are missing, and moreover, the thread for each button is old, so nothing was sewn on recently.

MICHEL. That is correct, but may I ask –?

POIROT. Mrs. Hubbard found this button in her room this morning.

MICHEL. *(Examining it.)* It is not mine, *monsieur.*

POIROT. So I see. But it matches yours exactly.

MICHEL. It does.

POIROT. Michel, are there other attendants on this train at the moment?

MICHEL. There is one in second class. A ticket taker I have known for years.

POIROT. Is he large or small?

MICHEL. Quite large, I'm afraid. Shall I ask him to see you?

POIROT. *Non, non,* that is quite all right. And what other passengers, besides the ones in this coach, are on the train?

MICHEL. There is hardly anyone at the moment. It is the off-season. There is a mother and child on the Belgrade carriage and that is all.

POIROT. And could there be a second conductor on this train wearing a uniform like yours?

MICHEL. Oh no, *monsieur,* there is no such thing. I had to earn this uniform with many years of service. However...

POIROT. *Oui?*

MICHEL. Well, frankly, I am not sure I trust her word, but Miss Ohlsson says that last night she saw what she calls a second conductor on the train.

POIROT. *(Suddenly alert.)* Miss Ohlsson?

MICHEL. *Oui,* she told me this morning.

BOUC. She did not tell *us* this morning.

MICHEL. She said he was wearing a uniform like mine and when she spoke to him he did not respond. In fact...

POIROT. What? *Tell me quickly!*

MICHEL. The princess tells me that she also saw this man last night.

POIROT. *Oh là là, oh là là, oh là là.*

BOUC. What is it?

POIROT. It is just the kind of clue that I have been waiting for.

> *(He springs into action.)*

Michel, come with me. I will need your help quickly. *Monsieur* Bouc, we shall be right back. Do not move!

BOUC. But where are you going?

POIROT. You will see in a moment!

> **(POIROT** *hurries out with* **MICHEL** *behind him – jostling* **MRS. HUBBARD,** *who is just entering.)*

MRS. HUBBARD. Ah!

POIROT. Pardon, *madame*! We will be right back!

MRS. HUBBARD. I thought you wanted to question me.

POIROT. I do! Just stay where you are!

> **(POIROT** *and* **MICHEL** *run out of the room.)*

MRS. HUBBARD. Well that was exciting – as if we needed any more excitement around here. Now listen, I want my passport back.

> *(She goes through the passports on the table, looking for her own.)*

What if there was another shooting and we had to make a run for it? Can you imagine me wandering through Yugoslavia without a passport? They'd shoot me on sight and ask questions later. *"Who are you?!"*

"Well I'm Mrs. Helen Hubbard from the Minneapolis Golf and Racquet *BLAM!*" No more mahjong!

BOUC. You have been extremely patient, *madame*, and believe me, I am grateful. If there is ever anything I can do to thank you, I am at your service.

>*(He kisses her hand.)*

MRS. HUBBARD. You know you remind me of one of my husbands.

BOUC. Which one?

MRS. HUBBARD. The next one.

>*(At which moment we hear **GRETA**'s voice from down the corridor.)*

GRETA. *(Offstage, approaching.)* No, no, no, please put it back! It is my suitcase! You may not take it!

>(**POIROT** *bursts into the room followed by* **MICHEL** *who is carrying a battered suitcase.* **MICHEL** *is followed by* **GRETA,** *the* **COUNTESS,** *and the* **PRINCESS.** **GRETA** *is hysterical and* **POIROT** *and the* **COUNTESS** *are trying to calm her down.)*

COUNTESS. He must have a reason.

POIROT. I have an excellent reason.

GRETA. Please stop!

PRINCESS. *Monsieur* Poirot, really!

POIROT. Miss Ohlsson, you must permit me to take a look in your suitcase.

GRETA. But they are private things! It has my undergarments!

PRINCESS. *Monsieur* Poirot!

POIROT. Miss Ohlsson, we will look at nothing that will embarrass you, you have my promise. Wait! I have an idea. Princess, would you be so kind as to assist me?

PRINCESS. I suppose.

POIROT. Miss Ohlsson: Michel tells me that you saw a second conductor on the train last night. Is that correct?

GRETA. *Ja.*

POIROT. And what did he look like?

GRETA. He vas small like a woman.

PRINCESS. That is correct. I saw him as well.

POIROT. *Ah bon,* that is perfect. It seems that virtually everyone on this train has seen the second conductor except myself and *Monsieur* Bouc. So the question now is where did he go. Is he hiding on the train? If he were still in uniform, we could spot him quickly. Therefore, at least one conclusion is that he has *hidden* his uniform and done so in the luggage of one of the passengers.

GRETA. But why choose me? There are other suitcases! Try the other ones first!

POIROT. *(The magician.)* Princess, would you be so kind as to raise the lid and tell us what you see inside?

> *(The* **PRINCESS** *raises the lid – and pulls out a uniform identical to the one that* **MICHEL** *is wearing.)*

COUNTESS. It is the uniform.

GRETA. Ahh! I haf never seen it! I have hurt no one, ever! I would not do such a thing!! I am not a murderer!!

POIROT. Oh now, now, now, I am not accusing you, you did nothing wrong.

GRETA. I did nothing wrong!!

POIROT. *Monsieur* Bouc, does the jacket have all its buttons in place?

BOUC. No. There is one missing.

MRS. HUBBARD. And there ya go! Are we surprised at this?

BOUC. Wait a moment. There is something more.

> *(He reaches into one of the pockets of the uniform and pulls out a large, distinctive-looking key.)*

BOUC. *Oh là là. Mon Dieu.* It is a pass key for the doors on the train.

MRS. HUBBARD. And *that* would explain how he got in my room.

> (**GRETA** *weeps loudly on the* **PRINCESS***'s shoulder.*)

POIROT. Now, now, *mademoiselle*, just tell me when was the last time you looked in your suitcase.

GRETA. It was yesterday, just after we boarded.

POIROT. So someone could have hidden it this morning after you left the room.

GRETA. *I have no idea! I have never seen it before!*

PRINCESS. *Monsieur* Poirot! I must insist that you stop bullying poor Miss Ohlsson in this manner. She is simply not up to it like the rest of us.

POIROT. You are right, forgive me. Now would you be so kind as to help Miss Ohlsson back to her room and take Mrs. Hubbard with you. I need to speak with the countess alone for a moment if you do not mind.

MRS. HUBBARD. Of course we mind. Every time things get juicy, you throw us out again!

PRINCESS. Uch. Would you please stop gossip mongering.

MRS. HUBBARD. Me? You have your mouth open so much I can count your teeth.

PRINCESS. What a pleasure to learn you know how to count. Bird brain.

MRS. HUBBARD. Well, if I'm a bird brain, you're a communist!

PRINCESS. I am not a communist, I'm in *exile*!

MRS. HUBBARD. From your *husband*, I'll bet, who couldn't wait *to get rid of you*!

PRINCESS. And who's the one with all the *divorces*?!

MRS. HUBBARD. My husbands were unfaithful!

PRINCESS. And this surprises you?!

BOUC. Ladies, ladies, we are all a little worked up at the moment – please. This way.

GRETA. Thank you.

> *(The* **PRINCESS** *and* **MRS. HUBBARD** *exit in high dudgeon. Everyone exits except* **POIROT** *and the* **COUNTESS**.*)*

> *(A moment.* **POIROT** *sighs deeply.)*

COUNTESS. You seem troubled.

POIROT. I am getting more and more concerned.

COUNTESS. That another crime will occur?

POIROT. No. That I will solve this one.

> **(POIROT** *picks up one of the passports and reads the contents.)*

Countess. What is your maiden name?

COUNTESS. Goldenberg. As you see in the passport.

POIROT. *Oui.* But now you use Andrenyi.

COUNTESS. My husband's name.

POIROT. Of course. The Countess Andrenyi. And I believe your first name is Eléna.

COUNTESS. That is correct. I am a suspect?

POIROT. I merely ask questions. That is my job.

COUNTESS. I thought we were friends.

POIROT. It is my greatest wish, but please indulge me. This morning I examined your passport and I saw a grease spot at the beginning of your name, Eléna. The spot occurs before the first letter, and it could easily hide another letter, such as H. Now if you add an H at the beginning of the name, it becomes *Helena*, which is used by Shakespeare in *A Midsummer Night's Dream*.

COUNTESS. That is true.

POIROT. The kind of name an actress might choose for her daughter.

COUNTESS. I suppose.

POIROT. An actress such as Linda Arden, the grandmother of Daisy Armstrong.

COUNTESS. If you say so.

POIROT. And the name Linda Arden is itself a stage name, surely. The word Arden was the maiden name of Shakespeare's mother and also the name of the forest in his play entitled –

COUNTESS. *As You Like It.*

POIROT. You know your Shakespeare well for a Hungarian.

COUNTESS. I have studied Shakespeare since I was a child.

POIROT. Yes, I know. I believe your mother Linda Arden taught it to you.

(*The* **COUNTESS** *is shaken but tries to hide it.*)

And that would make you the *aunt* of little Daisy Armstrong, the aunt who went to graduate school and got a degree in medicine, then moved to Europe and got married.

COUNTESS. (*A catch in her throat.*) I do not know this woman...

(*Sob.*)

But I would imagine that she still suffers from the loss of her niece and her sister.

(*She starts to weep quietly.*)

POIROT. My dear, there is no use denying it. When the train gets underway again and we reach the next city, a simple telegram will get me a photograph of Daisy's aunt and it will all be over.

COUNTESS. (*Suddenly without the Hungarian accent – purely American.*) But I didn't kill him! I should have but I didn't. I didn't even know who he was until you discovered it. But when you did, I realized that if you knew that I was Daisy's aunt, you would *think* that I killed him because he was...a *blackmailer*. And a *swine*! *And the murderer of a darling, sweet, innocent child who deserved to live!!*

POIROT. *Madame*, really –

COUNTESS. *It's the truth, I swear to God!* But I'll tell you this: If I had known who he was – that he was *Bruno*

Cassetti – the man who stole two of the people I loved most in this world – I would have pushed the dagger through his *chest myself, and believe me, no other wounds would have been necessary!*

> *(She stamps her foot in frustration – she is so angry she can't control herself – and she runs from the room in tears.)*

> *(**POIROT** is alone. He looks careworn and weary. We hear the agonized sounds of a solo cello once again, this time from the first movement of Bach's* Cello Suite No. 5 In D Minor. *And the lights dim.)*

> *(As we transition into the next scene, we see the **COUNTESS** in a corner of the train weeping from the depths of her soul.)*

Scene Four

(A moment later, **BOUC** *is seen at the end of the corridor, speaking into the radio transmitter.)*

BOUC. 'Allo, 'allo, can you hear me? I am calling Zagreb Station, can you hear me, Zagreb? This is Constantine Bouc of the Orient Express.

RADIO. *(Crackling.)* We are hearing you, *Monsieur* Bouc, you are loud and clear.

BOUC. We remain in the snowdrift in the Polinski Pass. Where are you?!

RADIO. We have been delayed, *monsieur*, but should reach you presently. How are conditions?

BOUC. We are losing heat and light, provisions are low, the passengers are angry and we have a dead man rotting in compartment two. How are things with you?

(We hear the allegro movement of Haydn's string quartet in D minor, Opus 76, No. 2. The lights cross-fade into the following scene.)

Scene Five

(In the transition, we hear all the suspects chattering away as they head for the dining car. When the lights come up, we are in the dining car and we see **ARBUTHNOT, GRETA,** *the* **PRINCESS,** *and* **MACQUEEN** *all waiting impatiently.)*

ARBUTHNOT. Well, I'd like to know what the *hell's* going on!

MACQUEEN. He wrote me a note and said to meet him here.

GRETA. He wrote me the same thing.

PRINCESS. I find this ridiculous!

> *(* **MRS. HUBBARD, MARY,** *and the* **COUNTESS** *enter from various directions.)*

MRS. HUBBARD. So where's that little Frenchman hiding? Is he being mysterious again?

MARY. He sent me a note to join him here.

COUNTESS. I received one also.

ARBUTHNOT. Well, he's obviously up to something, the little weasel.

> *(They all begin talking at once, "Do you think he solved it?" "Such an odd little man." "I wish this train would move already." "The man is ridiculous!")*

> *(At which moment,* **POIROT** *enters, followed by* **BOUC** *and* **MICHEL**.*)*

POIROT. *Pardon, pardon.* I have kept you waiting and I apologize. I had to get, how you say, my ducks in a row.

GRETA. Ducks? What ducks?

PRINCESS. It's an *expression*, Greta. You drive me crazy.

GRETA. Oh.

POIROT. Please all of you be seated, I have an announcement to make.

(They settle down and take a collective breath, then turn to **POIROT.** **POIROT** *takes center stage.)*

POIROT. Ladies and gentlemen. I have called you together in order to reveal to you the killer of *Monsieur* Samuel Ratchett, also known as Bruno Cassetti.

(They all react.)

MRS. HUBBARD. You're kidding!

PRINCESS. No!

ARBUTHNOT. I don't believe it.

MACQUEEN. You know who did it?

POIROT. I believe that I do. But first I must interrogate the last of your fellow passengers who has not yet answered any of my questions. Colonel Arbuthnot –

ARBUTHNOT. Me?

MARY. James?

POIROT. Do you have a problem answering my questions, *monsieur*?

ARBUTHNOT. No, of course not.

POIROT. Excellent. Now in the course of your service to your country, did you know an officer named Charles Armstrong?

ARBUTHNOT. No.

POIROT. Have you heard of him?

ARBUTHNOT. Yes, we served in the same theatre of action, but we never met.

POIROT. Have you heard of the Daisy Armstrong case?

ARBUTHNOT. Of course I have. She was murdered by some brute who was out for money.

POIROT. Did you know that Colonel Armstrong was Daisy's father?

ARBUTHNOT. No, I didn't.

POIROT. Or that he took his own life after the tragedy?

ARBUTHNOT. Oh God. I'm sorry to hear it.

POIROT. Colonel, at the hotel in Istanbul I overheard you say to Miss Debenham that you wished that she was out of all this. What did you mean?

ARBUTHNOT. I have no idea.

POIROT. Then *she* said that no one should see you together until it was, "All behind you." Until what was behind you?

ARBUTHNOT. I can't imagine.

POIROT. Are you aware that you are obstructing justice?

ARBUTHNOT. I am aware of no such thing.

POIROT. And you, *mademoiselle, c*an you explain what you meant?

MARY. I told you already. I wanted to get the *trip* behind me.

POIROT. I think you are lying.

ARBUTHNOT. Now listen here!

POIROT. Sit down, colonel, I am still talking. *Now tell me what you meant at the hotel! You wanted to get her out of what?! She wanted to get what behind her?!*

> (*They face each other squarely and the tension is high.*)

ARBUTHNOT. ... *I'm married!* All right?! I'm in the process of getting a divorce – which I deserve because my wife is seeing another man – but I'll lose my case in court if it's known that I'm seeing a woman socially. When the divorce is *behind us* we can stop hiding, which is why we've been trying to keep things *private*, no thanks to you!

POIROT. You have been doing a very poor job of it, I am afraid.

ARBUTHNOT. Well, some of us have emotions, Poirot. I'm sure you'd sacrifice your own mother if it led you to one of your damn solutions, and I don't think you know what the hell you're doing.

POIROT. I know exactly what I am doing, colonel. I am investigating the murder of Bruno Cassetti.

ARBUTHNOT. *Well, he deserved to die!*

POIROT. *Aha! Then you know who he is!*

ARBUTHNOT. Well...*yes*. They told me.

POIROT. But you did not know before they told you? And Colonel Armstrong was not your friend in the war? You did not save lives together as you fought with the Indian Army in the northern frontier?

> (**POIROT** *taps the ribbon on* **ARBUTHNOT***'s lapel.*)

You did not swear fidelity and friendship with this man at the time of your trial by fire together? *And now you do not give him the respect he deserves for all the tragedy and loss that he had to endure before he took his own life?!*

> (**ARBUTHNOT** *explodes with anger, grabbing* **POIROT** *by the lapel and lifting him off his feet.*)

ARBUTHNOT. SHUT UP YOU LITTLE CARPING NINNY! WHAT DO YOU KNOW ABOUT TRAGEDY, HAH?! WHAT DO YOU KNOW ABOUT HONOR AND LOYALTY AND YOUR GODDAMN JUSTICE!!

> (*Everyone springs up and tries to restrain him, overlapping.*)

BOUC. Stop!

MRS. HUBBARD. Colonel!

GRETA. Colonel Arbuthnot!

MARY. James!

PRINCESS. What are you doing?!

> (*For a moment we wonder if* **ARBUTHNOT** *will throttle* **POIROT** *and do him serious injury, but then he drops* **POIROT** *and turns away.*)

POIROT. You have been telling me lies, *n'est-ce pas*? Everyone in this room has been telling me lie after lie, but make no mistake. I know who killed Bruno Cassetti, and I know precisely how it was accomplished.

(*Silence.*)

MRS. HUBBARD. ... We're listening.

POIROT. The facts of the case could not be more simple. At five o'clock last evening this train left Istanbul on its way to Calais with stops in between. At approximately 12:30 last night, it ran into a snowdrift and was forced to stop. And at ten o'clock this morning, Mr. Cassetti was found dead with eight stabs wounds in his chest. These are the facts. *C'est tout. C'est fini!*

However...these facts permit two possible solutions to the crime. Under the first solution, one of Cassetti's enemies boarded the train at Sofia and brought with him a Wagon-Lit uniform which he later put on. Then, last night, using a pass key to enter Cassetti's compartment, he stabbed the man eight times and left through the door to Mrs. Hubbard's compartment.

MRS. HUBBARD. That's what I've been telling you!

MACQUEEN. Here, here.

BOUC. Well done, my friend. You have solved the case!

PRINCESS. Oh, I would not get too excited. He has not finished yet, have you, *monsieur*?

POIROT. No, princess, I have not finished. Let me propose a second solution because two unexpected events made the first solution impossible.

The first event was the snow which forced the train to stop: it meant that the killer now had a very big problem. *WHERE COULD HE GO?!* He could not get off at the next station *because there was no next station.* So unless the killer could *fly*, he must still be among us on this train. *He must be one of you!*

(*Silence.*)

MRS. HUBBARD. You said there were two unexpected events. We just can't wait to hear the other one.

POIROT. The second event was the discovery of the fragment of a letter that said, "Remember little Daisy Armstrong." And from this fragment we know that the killer was not some random enemy of Mr. Cassetti, but someone who came to avenge the death of a five year old child. Am I being fair about this, Miss Debenham? What do you think?

MARY. I... I suppose so.

POIROT. Excellent. Now with these facts in mind, the second solution took root, and little by little it has blossomed in all its terrible ruthlessness.

The first clue leading to this solution appeared within an hour of my arrival at Istanbul, when I learned that there was not a single ticket left on the first class coach of the Orient Express.

> *(Bang! Instantly, the room goes dark with only blue spotlights on the passengers as needed. This is a flashback to a moment earlier in the play, and the technique will recur again and again over the next few minutes.)*

BOUC. *(Flashback.)* It is never sold out at this time of year. That is ridiculous.

POIROT. And it *was* ridiculous. Why was this train so suddenly full? But thanks to *Monsieur* Bouc, I had a berth on the train, and soon, on the platform, I met an astonishing company of actors.

COUNTESS. *(Flashback.) Monsieur* Poirot, I look forward to hearing of your wonderful adventures.

MICHEL. *(Flashback.)* Princess Dragomiroff. How lovely to see you.

PRINCESS. *(Flashback.)* I have agreed to pay her way if she will assist me as I travel to Paris.

GRETA. *(Flashback.)* I am not married, except to God almighty who lives in heaven.

POIROT. Hungarian, French, Russian, Swedish. What were all these people doing on the same train? Something was amiss! It was like looking at a painting by Pablo Picasso. Over there is an eye, on top of an ear, behind a nose, *and nothing was normal*! Consider the moment in the corridor last night.

MRS. HUBBARD. *(Flashback.)* Help! Someone come quickly! Help!

BOUC. *(Flashback.)* Mrs. Hubbard. What? What is it?!

MRS. HUBBARD. *(Flashback.)* There was a man in my room! He ran off! I'm sure of it!

BOUC. *(Flashback.)* Which way did he go?!

MRS. HUBBARD. *(Flashback.)* That way! Just this second!

BOUC. *(Flashback.)* But *madame*, that is where I am coming from and I saw no one. How is this possible?

MRS. HUBBARD. *(Flashback.)* HOW SHOULD I KNOW!

POIROT. And then came the murder itself. A businessman dies in a locked room in a torrent of almost unspeakable violence.

>   *(Screeeeeeeeeeeech!! There is a sound of terror in the score.)*

GRETA. *(Flashback.)* Eeeee! Dear God, dear God, it is awful!

MACQUEEN. *(Flashback.)* Do you see his chest?!

PRINCESS. *(Flashback.)* It is horrible!

BOUC. *(Flashback.)* I cannot believe it!

POIROT. And then it was time to inspect the body, and the countess and I found not one, not two, but eight stab wounds to the chest.

COUNTESS. *(Flashback.)* Perhaps the man changed hands during the stabbing.

BOUC. *(Flashback.)* Or there were two assailants.

COUNTESS. *(Flashback.)* One strong, one weak.

POIROT. After that, I was offered a *feast* of clues! – The open window, the wine, the gun – until one clue of real importance was at last discovered: the broken watch.

COUNTESS. *(Flashback.)* It is stopped at 1:15.

BOUC. *(Flashback.)* Haha! At last! It is the time of death!

POIROT. But for me, the importance of the watch was not the *time* it told, but the place it was *found* – in Mr. Cassetti's pajama pocket, an unlikely place to keep a watch, don't you think? Do you sleep with your watch in your pajamas? Do you? Or you? Of course you do not, it would be uncomfortable, which led me to conclude that the watch was deliberately placed in the man's pocket so that I would think that the time of death was 1:15 – *a time when every single person on this train had an alibi*! But in fact Mr. Cassetti did not die until after *two o'clock when absolutely no one has an alibi*!

MRS. HUBBARD. You know I really don't think we need to be subjected to a performance like this in front of all the –

POIROT. SIT DOWN, Mrs. Hubbard. As for who actually killed Mr. Cassetti, the second real clue was found on the floor near the body – the handkerchief with the letter H in the fabric – and I now return it to its rightful owner, Princess Natalya Dragomiroff.

PRINCESS. But my name begins with an N, *monsieur*.

POIROT. Except that in Russian – in the Cyrillic alphabet, the letter N is written like the letter H in English.

(He presents it to her.)

PRINCESS. Thank you. I must have dropped it.

(She takes it.)

POIROT. And that leaves the most puzzling occurrence of the entire case.

MARY'S VOICE. *(Flashback.)* EEEEEEEE!!

(Bang!)

POIROT. As some of you will recall, I was speaking with Mrs. Hubbard and the colonel, when suddenly there was a scream and a gunshot –

MARY'S VOICE. *(Flashback.)* EEEEEEEE!!

(Bang!)

POIROT. But this was no ordinary scream and gunshot, my friends, this was a fabrication so *fantastic* and *elaborate* that for a moment even *I* was confused.

MARY'S VOICE. *(Flashback.)* EEEEEEEE!!

(Bang!)

ARBUTHNOT. *(Flashback.)* Oh my God! It's her!

BOUC. *(Flashback.)* What happened?!

ARBUTHNOT. *(Flashback.)* MARY?!

POIROT. Within moments of seeing Miss Debenham on the floor, I knew it was all a sham – a *performance*. How could a man only two feet away merely graze the victim in the arm, eh? And why would I find a powder burn on the sleeve of the blouse where the bullet entered? Because she fired the bullet *herself*, then dropped the gun, and fell to the floor.

ARBUTHNOT. Nonsense!

MARY. *I'd have to be crazy!*

POIROT. *Exactly! Crazy! That or committed totally to a course of action that meant everything to you.* Four people on this train were friends or family of Daisy Armstrong – do you not find this incredible?

MACQUEEN. *(Flashback.)* My father brought the case against that son of a bitch.

PRINCESS. *(Flashback.)* Daisy's grandmother is my dearest friend –

ARBUTHNOT. *(Flashback.)* He deserved to die!

COUNTESS. *(Flashback.)* I would imagine that she still suffers from the loss of her niece.

POIROT. And if there were four, could there be six or eight? Could Miss Debenham, not have been young Daisy's governess at the time of the kidnapping?

MARY. *(Flashback.)* I lived with a family for about a year. I'm a governess.

POIROT. And Greta Ohlsson who has been a baby nurse for years – may we not suppose that she was Daisy's nurse on Long Island?

GRETA. *(Flashback. She sobs.)* I am a missionary and I verk in Africa with little babies.

POIROT. As for Michel, it struck me from the beginning that a scheme like this could not be accomplished without someone on the *inside* – let's say a conductor who could come and go as he pleased. And then I recalled that the maid Suzanne who took her own life was from Paris, like Michel, and I wondered if this unfortunate girl was not Michel's daughter who went to work in America.

(**MICHEL** *covers his eyes and weeps.*)

And that leaves one last passenger on this train who is not accounted for – it leaves Mrs. Hubbard, who has certainly turned in the finest performance of the evening. It is not hard to see that she is an actress by profession, the grandmother of little Daisy Armstrong, the great Linda Arden, who has dazzled so many audiences during her distinguished career.

MRS. HUBBARD. *(Flashback.)*

THE BIRDS ARE SINGIN', IT IS SONG TIME

POIROT. Mrs. Hubbard, I salute you and assume that you masterminded the scheme from the beginning.

BOUC. *(To* **MRS. HUBBARD.***)* Is this true?

MRS. HUBBARD. *(Shrugs.)* I always wanted to be a director.

POIROT. And so, in the end, the murder was committed. There were eight stab wounds in the body. Some strong, some weak, some left-handed, some right-handed. And there were eight killers. You planned it together, you killed together, and in the name of justice you played God together.

(We see the murder now.)

(In a blue light of memory, each of the murderers plunges the knife into the body in front of him. Meanwhile we hear screech after screech of terror in the score.)

PRINCESS. For that little girl.

MICHEL. For my daughter, you pig!

ARBUTHNOT. For Charles!

MARY. For Daisy!

GRETA. For little Daisy!

MACQUEEN. For my father!

COUNTESS. For my darling Daisy!

MRS. HUBBARD. For my grandchild!!

> *(The effect is harrowing and liberating.)*

> *(When the ritual is over, the lights change back to normal and a level of peace is restored.)*

POIROT. And now, my friends, what am I to do? It cannot be long until the Yugoslavian police arrive, at which time I must tell them the truth, *n'est-ce pas?*

MRS. HUBBARD. You mean the truth, of course, about the second conductor.

COUNTESS. Anything else would be a complete injustice.

POIROT. On the contrary, it is the only justice. Under the law, if you commit a murder, you must pay the price.

ARBUTHNOT. But it was Cassetti who murdered the little girl!

POIROT. And did that give you a right to kill him?

ARBUTHNOT. *Of course it did!* He killed five people for some *ransom money.* And he'd done it before and he'd have done it again. And now it's time for you to turn around and walk away and leave us alone!

POIROT. *(Exploding.) No, it is not! It is not that time!* I have never in my life turned my back on the law! Do you understand that, colonel?! The law must be obeyed or we become *barbarians*! It is 1934, Europe is changing and there will be *chaos*! There will be nothing left of us and we will have to start again! *I cannot support this! I cannot agree to this*!

> *(Silence.)*

MARY. But the man was a monster, *Monsieur* Poirot. You know he was.

POIROT. But I cannot...

(*Beat.*)

I cannot just...

(*He is deeply moved.*)

MRS. HUBBARD. May a humble actress speak her peace?

PRINCESS. Please do, my dear.

MRS. HUBBARD. *Monsieur* Poirot, we are in your hands, and we acknowledge it. But would you really have preferred it if Bruno Cassetti had gotten away scot-free? Would that be the kind of justice you are after?

(**POIROT** *turns away.*)

Look at it this way: you have a complete solution staring you in the face. You have the button, you have the uniform, you have three reliable witnesses who saw a man in the corridor – and surely you're not calling all of us liars. Because if you did that...

(*Her tone changes.*)

There would be months of trials, lives would be damaged even more than they have been already, and a great many people would be forced to relive the most terrible moment in all of their lives – more terrible than any human being should ever have to experience. Is that what you want? Examine your heart and tell us what you want.

POIROT. ... You put me to the test, *madame*, and I am greatly troubled.

(*He turns to* **BOUC.***)*

Monsieur Bouc, my friend, you are the director of the Wagon-Lit. What do you say?

BOUC. In my opinion, the first solution you put forward is entirely correct: we had a deadly intruder disguised as a conductor, and I believe that is the solution you should offer the police.

(**POIROT** *hesitates. Then.*)

POIROT. *Alors.*

My friends.

May you go with God. And I hope that he gives you the strength you need to get on with your lives.

(*It takes a moment to sink in – then everyone starts to breathe again. They all start chattering with immense relief.* **MARY** *and* **ARBUTHNOT** *hug each other. Then so do* **MICHEL** *and* **MRS. HUBBARD**. *A cloud has lifted and they feel alive again.* "Oh, thank God." "It's a miracle!" "I thought it was over." "So did I!" "It's over!" Then.*)

(*Kerchunck!*)

(*The passengers are thrown forward as the train starts up again. They run to the windows and see the men outside.*)

BOUC. The crews have arrived!

COUNTESS. They are here at last!

MACQUEEN. Well, praise the Lord!

MARY. The train is moving!

BOUC. Thank God.

(**MARY** *bangs on the window, calling to the crew.*)

MARY. Hello! Hello, there! Thank you! Thank you so much! (*To* **ARBUTHNOT**.) Oh, James, do you see them?!

ARBUTHNOT. I told you we'd be all right in the end. You know, Poirot, you turned out to be more than I...

MARY. Poirot?

MRS. HUBBARD. *Monsieur* Poirot?

COUNTESS. He's gone.

MACQUEEN. Gone where?

BOUC. *Monsieur* Poirot?

> *(They look around. He's gone.)*

> *(Tableau.)*

> *(Then a light comes up on **POIROT** by himself.*
> *He speaks to the audience.)*

POIROT. And so the case was over at last, and the passengers went their separate ways. I have learned since that time that Greta Ohlsson did in fact get to Africa – for the first time, as it turned out – and she did work for the children and saved many lives. The colonel and Miss Debenham were married in a quiet ceremony in St. James Square, *Monsieur* MacQueen returned to his business, Michel to his trains, and the princess left us for the great beyond.

The countess, alas, went back to her husband, *Monsieur* Bouc and I have remained good friends, and Mrs. Hubbard – the great Linda Arden – has recently returned to the stage in a musical entitled *No, No, Nannette,* in which, I am told, she brings the audiences to their feet.

Meanwhile, I beg you to believe me when I tell you that I wish all of them well, and I hope that they prosper till the end of their days. But at night, in the darkness, when I am all alone, I ask myself again and again if this was justice; if I did the right thing. And on many such nights, it is not until morning that I can close my eyes.

> *(The lights fade.)*

> *(And then the lights are out.)*

End of Play